He'd known, eventually, they'd have to talk.

He was well aware of the conversations he'd avoided.

The wedding night he'd denied her.

Denied them *both*.

He'd prepared himself for the impact of her. The scent. The delicateness of her. The song of her voice in his ear.

But he wasn't ready.

She was anything but simple. But their situation was. A marriage to placate the people. A marriage on paper only.

Never for him.

"You haven't glanced at the diary," she said, "let alone asked what it is I—"

"I do not need to read a diary entry to tell you the answer is already no."

"It isn't a diary entry," she corrected. Dark brown hair fell about her slender shoulders. Her collarbone was so pronounced it sat like an adornment. Begging to be touched. Demanding his fingers smoothed along it and then up her pale neck.

Beautiful.

"And even if it were," she continued, "wouldn't you be curious?" The fluctuating flush to her cheeks deepened. Such a fascinating skill. To blush on demand. And oh, in another life, he would have tested that skill. "Aren't you curious about me?"

He was curious. That was the problem.

Lela May Wight grew up with seven brothers and sisters. Yes, it was noisy, and she often found escape in romance books. She still does, but now she gets to write them, too! She hopes to offer readers the same escapism when the world is a little too loud. Lela May lives in the UK with her two sons and her very own hero, who never complains about her book addiction—he buys her more books! Check out what she's up to at lelamaywight.com.

Books by Lela May Wight

Harlequin Presents

His Desert Bride by Demand
Bound by a Sicilian Secret

Visit the Author Profile page
at Harlequin.com.

Lela May Wight

THE KING SHE SHOULDN'T CRAVE

ISBN-13: 978-1-335-59332-0

The King She Shouldn't Crave

Harlequin Enterprises ULC
22 Adelaide St. West, 41st Floor
Toronto, Ontario M5H 4E3, Canada
www.Harlequin.com

Printed in U.S.A.

THE KING SHE SHOULDN'T CRAVE

Lisa, this one's for you. The middle child of two generations, this book is dedicated to you for all the reasons you know and some you never will. Love you. Always.

PROLOGUE

'AREN'T YOU AFRAID?'

'Never,' Princess Natalia La Morte soothed, despite the double beat of her heart and the hitch of her breath.

It wasn't fear making her skin clammy. It never had been. Because her future was preordained.

It was her fate.

The body getting into her bed was cold and Natalia shifted to be closer, wrapping her arms around a waist as slender as her own and holding her handmaid and friend close.

'I'm nervous.'

'Don't be, Hannah,' she told her, warming her up with gentle strokes of her open palms on her bare upper arms. 'We've done this a thousand times. *More.* It's the same as every morning.'

'It's not the same. Today you—'

'That's later,' she corrected. 'Not now. *Now* is the same. Later is—'

The future. And she'd been waiting twenty-one years for its arrival.

She cupped Hannah's cheek. The skin there was as cold as the rest of her. She met the blue of her wide eyes and reassured her with the steadiness of hers.

Because Natalia needed this. Today more than any other. This moment. This reminder of what she must do. And *why* she must do it.

'You will rest.'

'*Rest?* What if they come early? What if they discover—'

'They won't. They never have.'

Hannah nodded. 'Okay,' she agreed, lips pursed.

'Thank you.' Natalia closed her eyes and pressed her lips to Hannah's forehead. Her friend. Her confidante. Her jail-breaker.

Every morning she slipped from her bed and Hannah slipped into her place to become the Princess. To become *her*. And Natalia would do the opposite. She'd exchange her silk nightdress and soleless slippers for sturdy boots, trousers and a cloak of heavy wool, and then proceed to the next step of her morning ritual.

'I'll go,' she continued. 'But I *will* come back,' she promised. Because she would.

A life for a life.

It was what Natalia understood. Her mother's life had been the price paid to give her daughter life and every day she honoured her mother's sacrifice. Reminded herself of the debt she owed.

Natalia pulled the hood close to her cheeks. Hid the face her father had instructed the palace staff to protect at all costs and walked, unseen, through the palace. Through the winding halls and high ceilings that caused the smallest sound to echo off the marble floors.

Pretending, for a short time, that she wasn't the Princess any more, but only another member of staff. A staff member who rode the Princess's horse every morning because the Princess could only ever amuse herself in the palace grounds at a gentle trot. Never gallop. Never push. She should never exert herself. But all animals needed exercise. Needed to feel *free*.

Natalia slipped through an unguarded door to the gardens. Samson. Black as a raven's wing. Ready. Waiting. For her. For freedom. And she would let him taste it. *Feel* it.

Slipping her foot into the stirrup, she hoisted herself into the saddle and gave him a gentle kick. On cue, he trotted.

There were no bars in her prison, but it was a prison nevertheless.

It was a palace with sweet cherub faces mocking her from the highest turrets of dark grey stone with their faces full of whimsy. Idyllic. Safe. But there was always a border where she must stop. A barrier between her and the world. Between her and her people.

Her father's love—her father's grief—was her jailer. That was what kept her inside. Safe, as he had not kept her mother.

Freedom was an illusion.

She'd go back. She always did. Put on her dainty silk nightdress, slipped back into bed, watched her handmaid leave.

But Hannah wouldn't leave her today. They'd wait together for the circus to arrive. To pinch and pull and fold her body into folds of white silk. Prepare her for a promise made long before her birth.

Head bent low, she drove Samson faster, harder. He knew the way. Through the tall trees surrounding the palace grounds. Through the opening into the clearing.

Squeezing her thighs against hard muscle and snapping the reins, she urged him onwards to reach the same view they always did. The same destination. The top of the mountain path, where his gallop slowed to a heavy-hoofed stop.

And there it sat. On the horizon. Out of reach. Just as it had every day for twenty-one years.

Her destiny.

Camalò.

The palace was on the edge of the border separating two nations. Two kingdoms side by side, nestled in the heart of the Alps. Two mountain kingdoms of lush greens and snow-capped peaks piercing the sky-line. But that was where the similarity between the two kingdoms ended.

Vadelto, her home, was a prison of love and grief. Beautiful, underdeveloped and archaic. Camalò reeked of the future, tantalising her with of its newness like a book with a newly cracked spine. Roads wound into the mountains themselves, where white buildings with red roofs rose and fell on each new tree-lined tier of the alpine kingdom.

Her nation had been stuck in a time loop of regret because her father couldn't deal with his own grief.

Her mother had been the light, dragging her people and her kingdom from the Dark Ages, and when she'd died the light had been snuffed out. All the changes her mother had been implementing had stopped. The bor-ders had closed. The doors had been locked.

Her only chance to put things right…?

Marriage.

Today, she'd marry a king.

CHAPTER ONE

ANGELO DIZIENO KNEW the wrong man stood at the altar. The wrong twin. A man who should never have received the crown. A man who had forgotten his duty and abandoned his brother.

They'd shared a womb. Monochorionic-monoamniotic twins. Identical in *all* ways. Until life had separated them and stamped its differences on their skin.

Two minutes had separated their birth. One hundred and twenty seconds. Two sons. One heir…one spare. And an heir and a spare could never be the same. They'd both known it. Understood their roles.

Had understood them.

Bitterness crawled up Angelo's throat and sat on his tongue. His gaze swept over his audience. Pews full of European monarchs, diplomats, Prime Ministers…all waiting for him to show them he would not forget his duty again.

He was the King they needed, because he was the only King they had.

It was never meant to be this way.

It was never meant to be him.

And this was his punishment, wasn't it?

Marriage. Uniting two neighbouring nations because

of a promise made and set into a royal decree seventy-five years ago. Marriage to a princess who had been promised to his brother.

He couldn't help it—couldn't stop it. His top lip dipped in the centre to curl his mouth, because any second now they'd deliver a bride that never should have been his to his feet.

A bride whose face had lived in his mind for three long years. A bride he'd blamed for exposing him to the ugliness inside him and the extent of his resentment for being born the spare.

An acrid burn crawled up his throat. He sealed his lips, swallowed it down, buried it deep in his gut.

Just as you should have three years ago.

Angelo set his jaw, fixed his mouth, but regret cut deep. Because three years ago he should have looked away. Buried his feelings deeper. Pretended not to feel anything. Because he had not been himself. He'd been pretending to be the King. His brother.

They'd swapped places thousands of times before *that* day. Angelo had brokered many deals in his brother's stead, with charm and the grace of a royal. What was the difference in negotiating a decades-old treaty? Negotiating the terms of his brother's marriage?

Nothing should have been different.

Angelo had been better at those things, anyway. Better than Luciano at talking and teasing out the outcome they needed in diplomatic circumstances. They'd swapped places because Angelo was the better—

The better King?

He stiffened. His suit was too tight, too itchy.

What if...?

What a ridiculous *what if.* But it lingered. The regret.

What if he'd never gone inside her ugly castle, grey and dark, with its tall turrets and winding towers?

He sucked in a silent breath through his nostrils. He was lying. Her home had not been ugly. It had been enchanting, almost mystical. Ripped straight out of a fairy tale.

Her father, the old King, had pointed down to the gardens below, outside the arched windows of the tallest tower. A garden of tall, lush greens. And he'd seen her. The daughter the King wouldn't let the heir to Camalò's throne meet until their wedding day.

His reaction had been primal.

Mine.

The lush greens had trapped her inside a maze. This way or that? Did it matter? She'd seemed oblivious. Slowly, she'd walked. Her dress had been a deep purple. Her brown hair loose, untied, feathering across her shoulders and teasing at her waist. She'd touched the leaves of the bushes containing her, stroked them with gentle fingers.

And the recognition of her surrender had overwhelmed him.

She was just like him.

She was waiting to be summoned. Waiting for her father to tell her it was time to do her duty.

Charm had left him that day. He'd demanded the King's surrender to the inevitable. No choice. A promise of old. Their kingdoms *would* merge.

The King would keep the promise that their nations had set into a royal decree all those years ago. She would marry Luciano in three years' time, when she was twenty-one.

And that day had changed everything.

Because the mere sight of her had exposed what Angelo had already known but hadn't been able to voice. He'd wanted more than to pretend to be the heir to the throne. He'd wanted to *be* him. The heir. Not to take the crumbs of what the heir decided the spare could have. But to claim it all. Claim *her*. For himself...

The realisation of what he must do had been swift. He had to leave. Before his resentment became more than a heat inside him...became a fire that would destroy them both.

Angelo had severed all lines of communication. Cut himself free from anything and anyone that would keep him tethered to life inside the palace. He'd rejected the invisible bond between him and his twin. He'd rejected his duty to him because he was selfish.

And his exit from royal life had caused a riptide in the country's very foundations.

He'd left without preparation, with no transition for the people who needed him. No one to support his brother the way *he* had.

Now his twin was dead.

And the kingdom of Camalò was on its knees.

The country of his birth was falling apart at the seams, coming undone, because without him his brother had made all the wrong choices. The change to the dynamic had been too swift for him. Too fast. And everyone had suffered—all because he'd wanted *her*.

Angelo's neck snapped up as metal slid against metal and the smallest opening in the gothic arched doors at the other end of the aisle revealed his bride, dressed from head to toe in white lace.

Natalia La Morte.

His heart throbbed.

His blood roared.

Every muscle in his body pulsed. Hardened.

Duty demanded he didn't look away, didn't turn his back on her, but by God he wanted to. Every instinct told him to avert his eyes. Look away. But he had to look at her as a king and not as a man. Not as a human being with needs—wants. He had to look at her as he should have three years ago.

And there she was. Her face obscured by a veil.

He'd thought time would have dulled his reaction to her. Maybe he'd given his body's response to her too much credence. Too much blame for all the things that she'd exposed. Because it had already lived inside him, hadn't it? The bitterness?

And yet he wanted to see her face. Her lips. Her eyes. His body demanded it. The hands at his sides were threatening to reach out.

He flexed his fingers. Kept them loose and demanded they stay where they were. By his sides. *Still*.

But inside he was not still. He was restless. His skin itched…needing a lotion, a balm…

He couldn't drag his gaze away from the woman walking towards him. An innocent brought into the spotlight because this royal game needed her.

And she was getting closer.

White-tipped slippers peeked at him from beneath the layers of puffed fabric falling from her hips. Bringing her closer, step after step, along the red carpet. A bouquet holding an assortment of short-stemmed flowers was grasped between small, white-gloved fingers.

She was the catalyst of everything.

And now she was to become his queen.

He'd fulfil the old promise and join the two neighbouring countries. Marry her. What choice did he have? It was his duty now.

This long-awaited union of the two neighbouring countries would bring peace to an unsettled nation, wouldn't it? Show the people that their new king would do what should be done. Follow the path already set and be the leader they needed.

The leader his brother should have been. *Could* have been if Angelo had stayed.

The Princess moved to stand in front of him. A warm wash of floral aromas clung to his nose, smothering his pores with the heady scent of all that had been forbidden to him.

His hands stopped obeying his command. They reached out…pinched feather-light fabric between his fingers, and he curbed his instinct to reveal her face swiftly.

Slowly…oh, so slowly…he lifted the silk away from the tip of her pale chin, away from her lips, her rosebud mouth, to reveal her eyes.

His hands stayed where they were, frozen at her temples, but the veil fell from his fingers, gliding over her diamond-encrusted tiara to fall down her back.

Lagoon-green eyes pulled him in and under. Trapped him. Bewitched him as they had three years ago. Lust speared through him. Flowed through his veins in a gush.

She was everything he remembered. Her curled lashes. The wideness of her eyes. The deep dip between her full upper lip and her long, up-flicked, haughty nose, all enclosed in an oval-shaped face.

Beautiful…

But it wasn't her beauty that had stayed with him.

Or it wasn't *just* her beauty. It was what she was. What the royal game had turned her into. Turned *him* into. A royal pawn.

It was a similarity he had never shared with his twin, and yet he shared it with her. Silently. In the shadows. And he'd wanted to drag her into the light three years ago. Play with her in their own game instead of being the royal pawns they were. Pieces to be moved around to suit a monarchy older than time.

They had both been waiting for duty to summon them…demand their obedience.

They would be obedient now.

They would follow the rules.

Slowly, he made his hands move. He pulled them away from her face.

Fire, hot and unrelenting, licked at his insides as his fingers accidentally grazed her skin. Feathered across a tiny ear, lifted the taut skin of her neck. And he couldn't help it. He let his fingers linger, moved them down the column of her throat…

What are you doing?

He dropped his hands to his sides. Refused to clench them to stem the burn thrumming in his palms, his fingertips.

His brother's promised princess.

Once forbidden, now his for the taking…

He turned his attention to the priest and nodded. He refused to acknowledge the woman in his peripheral vision any longer. Ignored the need demanding he look at her again. Ignored the hammer of his heart demanding he ease the need.

He focused on all the eyes burning into his back.

Duty had summoned them both, and he'd do his.

He'd marry her. Fulfil the brother's promise. And then he'd set her aside. *Forget her.* Focus on what mattered. The only things that *could* matter.

His duty to his brother's memory.

His duty to the crown.

His people.

What about her?

A prick of pain pierced through his temples.

It was guilt.

She was so small beside him. Standing so close he could feel the warmth of her through his suit.

His fingers flexed, urging him to clasp the hand she had not knotted around her bouquet in a death grip, to reassure her—

Of what? That she isn't alone?

She *was* alone.

Just as he was. Alone in a room full of strangers.

And that was what they would remain.

Strangers.

He didn't owe her anything other than what he'd promised. A ring, a royal wedding, a new name, a union of their nations. That was exactly what he'd give her. And after—

His breath snagged in his throat.

Nothing came after.

Nothing but duty.

The priest's lips were moving, but Natalia couldn't hear him. Only the whoosh in her ears. The thud in her chest.

Her skin throbbed. Pulsed. She wanted to touch it. Run her fingers down the column of her throat. Touch where his fingers had brushed. Evoke the feeling that had burst to life in her chest. Stilted her breath. It had been a heat. A yearning to raise her hand and touch his skin, too. To look into his honey-brown eyes the way he'd looked into hers.

Beneath the layers of white silk, she trembled. Her body, her every muscle, was tight. Taut. As if she'd just ridden her horse hard into the mountains.

Was it attraction?

Was this what it felt like?

She straightened her shoulders, focused on the priest, on his aged hand hovering above the holy book.

It was the unexpectedness of the Prince that was riding her senses. That was all, wasn't it?

She'd been betrothed long ago to a man she'd never met because her father had not permitted their meeting. He hadn't seen the point. Not until she was of age. Not until her wedding day.

There had been no pictures, no letters of correspondence, no secret meetings in the dark or even in the daylight to form a connection. Nothing but words from her father confirming that her fate was sealed.

It was her duty.

She was the first daughter born in over half a century.

She was promised.

The union would keep her protected when her father could not.

And it hadn't mattered to her. Not the lack of communication. Not the lack of knowing the man she would marry. She'd only cared that she would marry the King in the palace just beyond the border of her kingdom.

Every morning, looking at that palace over the border, she'd felt that her destiny wasn't a man. It was the crown he would enable her to claim.

The people sat behind her. Watching her.

They were the source of the adrenaline pinching her nipples into tight buds. They were causing the dryness of her throat.

Why was it so dry?

She swallowed.

Focused.

And yet the man standing to her left clawed at her senses. His scent was floral, with powerful notes of something earthy. Almost bitter. Like earth, newly kicked up by a horse's hooves. The scent of adventure…

She *knew* that scent.

It wasn't the man exciting her, but what he offered. Everything she'd been waiting for. *Release.* For this promised marriage was to open the gates to her prison.

Well, she was outside now. And she was ready to marry the man beside her so she could become a queen, because some rule said she needed to.

'Your Highness?' The priest's grey eyes were fixed on hers expectantly.

What had she missed?

He dipped his head. 'Your gloves.'

She looked down at the intricate lace sheathing each finger.

A warm pressure on her waist drew her gaze. Fingers against white satin. Such elegant fingers. Such power in their gentle caress.

She lifted her head, met his eyes. They were intent on her. Watching her. She saw a face made of sharp lines. A noble nose. A square jaw shadowed by a well-groomed beard.

'Allow me.'

His voice was a low husk. A command. And her heart thumped as her hand obeyed. Stayed still.

He loosened each gloved fingertip on her left hand. Her whole focus shifted and locked on to the olive fingers working on hers. The contact was so casual, yet so intimate. He tugged the lace over her wrist to feather the sensitive dip in her palm. Continued upward. Between her fingers, exposing her knuckles.

He stripped her hand bare. Dropped the glove to the floor. And she couldn't breathe as he turned her hand over and placed upon the tip of her finger a gold band.

The symbol of their union.

'Ready?'

The question penetrated her core. Released a rumble in her gut. Her eyes lifted to his. Deep and steady, they held hers. Not rushing her. Not urging her to hurry. Not reminding her that there were a thousand other people in the room. He waited for her answer. Waited for *her*.

She wasn't alone in this, was she?

She'd never considered the man behind the Camalò crown. Only *her* crown. When she was given it, she would be Queen. Her father would step aside, and she would become head of state. But there were two people here. Two kingdoms being merged by one royal marriage.

Was she ready?

They'd all been waiting for this moment. Her nation had been in mourning for twenty-one years because her father could not let go of his grief. Her mother's death had halted everything.

It was time.

Change was coming. *Again*.

Love would never derail her nation again.

She would wake them all up, as her mother had. She would bring the change her mother would have had she lived.

She would pay off the debt she owed because her mother had died bringing her into the world.

A life for a life.

Natalia.

A queen for the people.

And *only* the people.

'I'm ready.'

The priest's voice leaked into the bubble surrounding them, but in a room full of people she could only see *him*.

Her promised king.

'Do you, Angelo Dizieno, King of Camalò, take Natalia La Morte, Princess of Vadelto, to be your lawfully wedded wife?'

His gaze, firm and intense, held hers, and she couldn't look away. 'I do.'

'Do you, Natalia La Morte, Princess of Vadelto, take Angelo Dizieno, King of Camalò, to be your lawfully wedded husband?'

Here it was. The moment that would seal her fate. As was preordained. As was her destiny.

'I do.'

The gold band slithered down her finger.

'You may now kiss the bride.'

His dark head dipped, and she sucked in a breath. Her face felt frozen, waiting for contact with him. For the final seal on their destiny.

She braced herself. Shoulders squared. Spine straight. She fought the urge to close her eyes and watched his flicker shut. Obscenely long lashes fluttered closed as he moved in. His breath mingled with hers. Hot. Sweet. *Masculine.*

His lips were so close, so near. She moved on instinct, rising on the balls of her feet. She was closer. Placing her hand on his broad shoulder.

He moved in the final millimetres. The hair on his top lip brushed against hers. A tickle. A caress. The pressure of his mouth increased. Firm, but also featherlight.

And the raging butterflies in her chest swarmed through her body to meet the caress of his lips.

And her body sang. Hummed. *Electrified.*

Her heart hammered, and the moment was over before she could analyse her body's response. Its reaction.

He raised his head a fraction and swept in to place his mouth to her ear.

The butterflies danced.

'It is over, Principessa.'

Her brow furrowed.

Hadn't it only just begun?

CHAPTER TWO

Two months later...

NATALIA FINGERED THE silverware placed with merciless precision. The gleaming blue and white patterned plate, seemingly untouched by human hand. No smudges, no imprints of careless fingers, no evidence of life.

She placed her hand in the centre of the plate and pressed down. She inhaled, exhaled, counted to ten, and lifted.

There. Life. Creases and folds unique to her. *Proof.* She wasn't invisible.

So where was he? For two months, every evening, she'd made the same request. An audience with the King. Every time they'd denied her. *He'd* denied her.

Still, she waited.

She'd swapped one palace prison for another. Another holding cell full of silver spoons and fine porcelain. She was free to roam the grounds, and all over the palace. Except the west wing. The old Queen's quarters were off-limits to her.

As was the King.

She'd had two months to explore the palace. Eight weeks to realise the extent of his abandonment.

Separate quarters. Separate beds. *Separate lives.*

She was as alone as she ever had been. Alone in this. This facade of a marriage.

But what had she expected to happen?

She hadn't thought about it at all. She'd assumed things would be different. *She* would be different.

Her cheeks heated as she swallowed down frustration at her naivety.

Time was running out. One week remained until her coronation. One week until she became Queen. And every day her dream seemed further away. Every day in her new home she was thwarted by rules. Tradition. Her every request denied without the permission of the King.

The man who'd brushed his lips against hers in a kiss she hadn't been able to forget.

Hands appeared to her left and silently tried to change her plate.

'Leave it!' she demanded and added, 'Please,' because they were only doing their job. Removing any evidence that she was there.

'Your Highness.'

The hands disappeared. But not the smudge. The proof.

She raised her gaze to the opposite end of the highly polished rectangular table. Her eyes moved past the gentle glow of flickering candles. His chair was empty. No fine china set before it—no silverware—no proof of life.

But she knew he lived. She remembered the press of his mouth. The glow of his honey eyes…

The door opened. The King's private secretary appeared, a neutral expression on his face.

She stood and stopped his approach with an open palm. There would be no whispers in her ear tonight.

'Surely the King must eat?' she asked, breaking protocol, breaking the rules to stay quiet and wait.

'His Majesty sends his apologies—'

She shook her head. She knew his choice to eat without her was a statement. A declaration. That her presence—*their marriage*—was inconsequential.

Realisation stormed through her. Of what her life would continue to be if she let it. Hidden from her duty. Ignored. Dismissed. Her mother's dreams forgotten. Her people left behind.

'Take me to him.'

'Your Highness…' He shook his head. 'I cannot,' he said, denying her, like everyone else.

'Then I will find him myself.'

His eyes widened. 'The King—'

'Will no longer ignore his wife.'

She moved past him, hating her rudeness, but what choice did she have? She couldn't wait any more. She was running out of time. She could ask the myriad of staff to help her with her coronation speech, but only he could approve it.

She blocked the personal secretary's attempts to overtake her as she moved through the halls. The portraits seemed to tut their disapproval from their allocated frames. But she didn't care. Not for the rules. Not for tradition.

Natalia stopped at the door to his study. His hideout. Shoulders locked, back straight, she pushed open the old oak door—and there sat the King.

Her tight lungs urged her to inhale deeper, but she

couldn't. He mesmerised her. The presence she'd questioned was real.

Dark hair raked to the side kissed his earlobes and his proud forehead. A strand fell helplessly in the centre to sit at the top of his nose. A noble nose. And such full lips...

Her gaze travelled down his exposed throat to the open collar of his black shirt. To the V where a smattering of fine dark hairs peeked at her. Urging her to feel them. To test the softness beneath her fingers.

Her gaze shifted slowly across the breadth of his chest to his broad shoulders, to arms so wide...

His pen halted mid-swipe, held between long fingers, balanced by a thick wrist cuffed in black. His eyes rose from the paper in front of him.

Lashes, full and long, captured a sunset of liquid gold.

A hypnotising swirl of heat locked on to her. A warmth spread through her fingers, through her arms, her chest, to pump into her stomach. *Lower.*

Everything stopped—including time.

He stared at her.

She swallowed.

She didn't want to recognise him as a man. With this heat in her gut. Because whatever this womanly response was, she didn't like it. It had no purpose here. In this room. *With him.*

'I need to speak with you,' she said huskily, before her training could stop her. Before it demanded she stand silent and continue to live her life like a puppet. Her strings pulled by men. By tradition. By the rules that only served the King. Not the people. Not *her*.

Angelo lowered his gaze. 'Then make an appointment.'

His olive fingers flicked over the white paper. Dismissing her.

'Your Majesty...' The aide she'd forgotten swept into the room. 'I apologise—'

'Leave us,' he said, his eyes settling back on Natalia, and his look was as blatant as his actions since their wedding. He didn't want her here.

The door closed. Leaving them alone for the very first time.

'Why are you here, Principessa?'

Honey-brown eyes latched on to hers. Her breath hitched. The words—all the words she'd held back—swarmed and clumped in her throat.

She'd demanded his attention and here he was, giving it to her.

He was waiting for her to respond.

What was she waiting for?

Her training told her she shouldn't say a word. Should apologise for interrupting him and leave. Speak only when spoken to. But her obedience had been a facade. The long game. A cover-up.

Uninvited, she reached for the chair opposite him and sat down. Placed her hands in her lap and straightened her back.

Her fingers curled into her palms, her nails biting into her skin. This was the moment. *Her moment.* And it would hurt to let her underbelly show. To loosen her armour. But what choice did she have other than to tell the truth? To make this an unguarded moment of honesty?

She couldn't do this alone. The gates were still locked against her, and the shackles of tradition were too tight for her to free them by herself.

She swallowed, pushing down the instinct not to

speak. Not to tell him the truth. But she had nothing to lose and everything to gain.

'I need your help.'

Her armour cracked. And it hurt. The confession in her mouth was heavy, but she made herself push it out. Set it free.

Natalia reached into her pocket and withdrew her coronation speech. She unfolded it with careful precision, leaned forward and placed it before him.

'And I'm not leaving until I get it.'

No one needed him.

That's a lie, isn't it?

Angelo gritted his teeth. 'Needs are precarious, *Princess*,' he bit out in English, emphasising the difference in their positions. Their status.

She was a queen-in-waiting. He was already king of all he surveyed.

His gut kicked.

'Read it.'

Her voice was pure silk. It feathered over his skin, encouraging each fine hair to stand on end in its wake. And it chafed.

'No.'

He pushed an unsteady hand through his hair. Refused to look down at the paper with its square folds and cursive penmanship. It was written by her hand. Not on a computer. Not by an aide who'd taken notes from words said by her lips. Whatever it was, she'd obviously kept it hidden in her pocket. Close to her body.

It was personal. And he had no intention of becoming personal with her.

He'd known that eventually they'd have to talk. He was well aware of all the conversations he'd avoided.

The wedding night he'd denied her.

Denied them *both*.

He'd prepared himself for the impact of her. The scent of her. The delicateness of her. The song of her voice in his ear.

But he wasn't ready for her. Not in a long, simple shift dress, with oversized buttons leading from the V beneath her collarbone to her feet.

She was anything but simple. But their situation was. Theirs was a marriage to placate the people. A marriage on paper only.

'You haven't glanced at it,' she said, 'let alone asked what it is. I—'

'I do not need to read a diary entry to tell you my answer is already no.'

'It isn't a diary entry,' she corrected.

Dark brown hair fell about her slender shoulders. Her collarbone was so pronounced it sat like an adornment. Begging to be touched. Demanding his fingers smooth along it and then move up her pale neck.

'And even if it were,' she continued, 'wouldn't you be curious?'

The fluctuating flush in her cheeks deepened. Such a fascinating skill. To blush on demand. And, oh, in another life he would have tested that skill.

'Aren't you curious about me?' she asked. 'The woman you married? The woman you've put on the other side of the palace from you and have forgotten about for two months? Don't you want to get to know me at all?'

His lips compressed and jutted forward as he rolled his distaste inside his mouth.

Was it shame lingering on his tastebuds? Bitterness tainting his saliva because she was calling him out on his obvious abandonment?

Did he care if it was?

No, he would not acknowledge it. Whatever it was. But he'd forgotten nothing and he *was* curious. That was the problem.

He wanted to know her. *Intimately.* She was a fever dream he couldn't escape. Even in a palace as big as this.

'No,' he lied, without missing a beat. Without a flicker of *anything.* He flattened his palms on the desk. He'd tame his desire. Stunt it. *Forget it.*

But his body mocked him. Defied him. Because his reaction was instant. The hard, throbbing length of him luckily concealed beneath his desk.

'Why wouldn't you be curious about your future queen?' she asked, her eyes flitting between both of his. 'Your wife?'

'Because I don't need to know you, Princess. Surely you are not so naive?' His brows pinched together. 'You understand what you have married into, don't you?' he asked. Because hadn't he made it clear? For both their sakes, he didn't want to know her. Didn't want to cross any boundaries. They would remain strangers. Nothing more between them than the titles of King and Queen.

He didn't want to cross any boundaries with her.

He'd left her alone, avoided her every day since their spectacle of a wedding, to stamp into her brain what their marriage involved.

Her eyes darkened. 'I understand what this marriage means to *me*.'

He bit down on the inside of his cheek. This entire conversation was futile. But maybe she needed the message that he was unavailable to her to be spelt out. Clearly.

'Do you want to know what this marriage *actually* means for you?' he asked. Because hadn't he always wished he'd had things spelt out for him before he'd left? The significance of his role in the monarchy? What walking away from his role would do to his brother? The people? The kingdom?

Lips pursed, she nodded.

'Our marriage is an empty symbol of union,' he said. Because it was the truth. He *was* empty. He had nothing for her. This was it. 'It means nothing more than what our ancestors promised and what my brother and your father agreed to. A union of two nations promised before our time,' he explained. 'A marriage for the people. For duty.'

'I understand what duty is. The duty I have to my people as I come into this marriage,' she said. 'I also understand we don't need to have a relationship to be King and Queen and for our nations to merge.'

Her throat constricted and so did his gut. The urge to place his hands on her shoulders and ease the tension stormed through him.

'You're correct,' he agreed. 'We don't.'

He hardened himself to her. To this woman telling him she needed his help. Seeking him out and demanding it. He couldn't help her. Whatever it was, he didn't care.

And he wouldn't pretend he did. He wouldn't pretend

to be something he wasn't, as he had with his brother. He'd given Luciano an illusion that he would always be there. By his side. Supporting him. Holding him up. Selfless. But he wasn't selfless, he was greedy...a crown-stealer.

'I understand,' she said. And, oh, how fluidly her lips moved around the word, pushing it between her teeth in emphasis. 'Even to make babies in order to continue the royal line of succession we don't need to become an "us". You can continue to pretend I don't exist until the time comes for us to conceive an heir.'

Heir. The word echoed in his mind, raising his core temperature. And following it came the word *spare.*

'And even then,' she continued, her voice throaty, 'we'd only have to meet in my most fertile periods. We are both young. Hopefully we have many fertile years left—'

'Your point?' he interjected when the throb between his thighs began to hurt.

Her eyes widened. 'You owe me nothing,' she reassured him.

'Exactly,' he drawled, with a confidence he didn't feel.

He did owe her something. They were both in this position because of him. She should be brother's wife. His brother's queen. And yet here she was. *His.*

Natalia's eyes flicked to the paper on the desk between them. He watched the slide of her forehead, the elegant shape of her nose. Her head swung back to him, drawing his attention to her long throat, the sway of hair across her shoulder.

He curled his fingers into his palms.

'But I owe my people everything,' she said. 'Read it, please.'

Please. Such a simple word. A powerful one.

He blew out an agitated breath. His plan to abandon her, to leave her to her own devices, wasn't working, was it? Because she was here, in front of him, begging him to take notice and refusing to leave until he did.

He made his body still. Made it not react. Made his gaze lift. Made himself meet her eyes, glistening with determination.

The Princess was not content to be left alone—and she wasn't leaving, was she?

The message wasn't getting through to her. The same way his lust was not diminishing as it raced through his body.

He couldn't have her. Not the way he wanted to.

He wanted to get down on his knees and raise her skirt. To find the heart of her he longed to taste.

She's not for your tasting!

He reached for the slip of paper on his desk.

It was only five hundred or so handwritten words.

What would the harm be in placating her if it would make her leave? Leave him alone?

He stood, picked up her offering. Toe to heel, he moved his feet purposefully around the desk. He raised his hand, watched her eyes widen, her mouth thin, as she looked at the paper between them.

'Read it to me, Principessa.'

She shifted in her chair, leaned over just a fraction, and it released a wave of her scent.

He closed his nostrils and breathed through his mouth. And that was a mistake. Now he could taste her. Something subtle. Floral. Sweet. Everything he wasn't.

He released the piece of paper to her and sat on the edge of the desk, facing her. 'I'm waiting,' he said—because he was. Waiting for this unnecessary meeting to be over.

'Before I read it...' She placed the paper on her lap and moved her hands over it, smoothing the folds. She looked up. 'Do you know what my life is like here?'

'Of course I do,' he said, keeping his position on the desk. Ankles knotted, palms on his thighs, he held her gaze. 'I live here.'

'And so do I,' she countered.

He would not respond. Would not tell her how every day was a hard-won battle for him to forget that she did.

'Do you know what my life was like before I arrived here?' she continued when he didn't respond. 'What life is like in Vadelto?'

Her question was a right hook to the gut. A reminder of how shut-off she'd been—not only from the world but even from her neighbouring country. And he'd positioned her in his palace and closed the doors behind him. Without thinking. Without care.

Just as you did with your brother.

This was nothing like the way it had been with his brother. With his brother, he'd promised to support him. With her, he would not offer the same. His country was all that mattered to him now. His people.

'Should I care?' he asked, despite the hollow in his gut. 'You don't live there any more. You live here.'

'But I might as well still be living there, because nothing has changed.' Perfectly arched brows pinched together above narrowed eyes. 'I wake up. I'm washed and dried. Someone moisturises my skin from my toes to my forehead. I'm dressed like a porcelain doll and I'm treated like one.'

'Then don't behave like one,' he said, before he could stop himself. 'If you want a bath, take one. Brush your own hair. You don't need my permission to decide how you manage your beauty regime.'

'That's not what I meant. I'm trying to explain the reasons behind why I'm here. Why I've come to you. Because even with my coronation in sight, I'm still trapped by tradition.'

'There are no quick exits from royal expectation,' he said, because there weren't.

'Apparently I can't leave the palace grounds until I'm Queen. I'm not allowed to have access to the outside world until after my coronation. Some stupid rule, written decades ago, says that a prince's bride must wait to meet the people. Wait until she's Queen before she can claim any type of free will. And even then her king is her master.'

'Master?' he repeated. 'I do not want you to serve me.'

'The rules are the same for any Vadelton princess. Tradition dictates I follow your lead. Follow the rules. Unless you—'

'Unless I what?'

'Change them.'

Her words caught at his breath. He'd left Camalò seeking change, because change was not to be had at home, and he'd been tired of being invisible. *Second-best.*

His brother had passed away because of his choice to cause change, even though it hadn't been required.

'Change is inevitable. You're here, aren't you? That *is* change.'

She dipped her head. Her hair fell over her shoulders and, goddamn him, he wanted to push it back. Keep her creamy skin…that defined collarbone…exposed.

Shoulders back, spine straight, she raised her head and held out her little piece of paper again. 'This is my coronation speech.'

He kept his hands where they were. 'And what does it say, Princess?'

'It explains what it is I'll do.' She placed it down again when he didn't take it. 'What I *want* to do as Queen.'

'And what is that?'

'Free my people.'

'Are they prisoners?' he asked. 'Your borders have been closed for my lifetime. You are a self-sufficient nation.'

'We are a backward nation.'

'Royal life is not a fairy tale. We do not all clap our hands, shouting, *We believe!* in the hope that things will come to pass in the blink of an eye.'

Her chin jutted out. Such a determined chin. Such elegance in the motion.

He sucked in a silent breath through flaring nostrils.

'I'm not clapping,' she corrected. 'I'm talking. And I will keep speaking until my people have freedom. Until *I* can give it to them.'

'What is it you wish to change?'

Her beautiful features twisted into a grimace. 'I want them to be able to drive. Have access to real education. Not just rudimentary education. So they can keep my country self-sufficient. I want them to work not only for their country, but for themselves. I want them to *want* education that grows not only their minds but their souls. I don't want to only touch my people's lives economically. I want to touch their spirits. Their hearts.'

'A true fairy tale princess?' His veins bulged. 'Ridiculous.'

He shook his head because he knew the truth. Her words were simply a cover-up. She was just tired of being invisible.

'My dreams for my people are not ridiculous,' she said. 'I want my people to know what I intend to do for them when I become Queen. I want more for my people. Not for myself.'

He knew exactly what she wanted. Because he'd wanted it too. *Once.* He recognised her truth even if she didn't.

He stood, closed the distance between them, watched as she dragged in a lungful of air when he entered her proximity. 'I will read your speech.'

She handed it to him.

He read her grand plans for soaring towers of education, roads, import, export, tourism, ships, hotels—everything Camalò already had, she wanted to achieve with a click of her heels.

He placed it face down on his desk and turned to her. 'Your speech will scare them,' he told her. 'It is too much, too soon.'

She stood. 'Scare who?' Her brows pinched together. 'You?' Her hands clenched at her sides. 'Fear has deprived my people for decades.'

And he heard it. The hiss of her unspoken words. *Fear has deprived me.*

'Fear won't dictate my reign as Queen,' she continued with a gush of air. 'Change—'

'Change must be organic,' he interrupted. 'Not dramatic. Because when they put that crown on your head there will be no need for your cries for change. The people will already see it happening. Change *is* happening. All you have to do is wait for it.'

'I'm tired of waiting.'

She side-stepped him, and it was like a drag on his senses as she moved away. She paced. The blue rug beneath her feet compressed with each hurried step.

'My mother wanted the same changes I do.' She wrung her hands as her pacing quickened. 'She convinced my father to open the borders. To bring outside life into our world. Grant uninhibited access to the internet.'

She paused, pulled her bottom lip between her teeth. Bit at the plumpness. Nibbled it.

He hated himself at that moment. She spoke of her mother, and yet he was hard. Painfully so. And it hurt.

'And yet *you* don't want uninhibited access to the internet. Why not?' he asked.

Despite his need to distance himself from her, he had been so very grateful that she'd simply said, *'No, thank you,'* when presented with a laptop and her own study. Because he was glad the record of the debauched lifestyle he'd had when he'd left the kingdom could not be on her radar.

But for how long?

Did it matter? Why did he care if she read all the leaked kiss-and-tell stories of his nights, weekends, weeks of depravity, spent in bed with multiple brunettes with pale skin and plump pink lips?

They all resemble her, don't they? You couldn't have her, so you had everyone who looked like her instead?

No. He'd left and had the lifestyle only permitted to the spare to the throne. A life that had been his for the taking. Taking whatever he could. Wherever he could. It had been his due for being born second. Or so he'd thought. He'd been reckless with himself. With his country. With Luciano…

All of it all came back to him.

The heaviness of regret.

He was a selfish bastard.

'Just because I don't want it for myself, it doesn't mean my people shouldn't have it,' she said, pulling him back into this conversation he'd never wanted to have.

He'd wanted her to fall in line. Follow his lead without question. Without disruption. Do her duty. *Silently.* But here she was. Disrupting the status quo.

'I would never ask you to withhold it from them,' he replied—because he wouldn't. That had never been his intention. He knew her country's dynamics would have to change. 'I will not withhold growth from your people, but I don't understand why you would withhold it from yourself?'

'I have my books. I have all I need without seeing the world outside our kingdoms. I want balance here at home. I don't need to look beyond our borders to know what needs to be done. My mother planned it all,' she said, pulling him out of his wanton haze, his self-disgust. 'She wanted to put in roads…an infrastructure to accommodate more than a few state cars, to bring tourism. More. My mother is a legend to my people. She was—'

'Everything you want to be?'

'I could never be her,' she dismissed. 'But she died

bringing me into this world and I owe it to her. I owe it to my people to give them everything that was stolen from them because of me.'

He couldn't speak. The blood in his veins whooshed in his ears. It was as if they were mirror images, the same... The snap of a puzzle being completed—

No.

'You can help me break the chains of tradition,' she said. 'You can help me change the rules.'

'No.'

Her face fell, and so did his stomach. But he continued anyway.

'I do not want change, dramatic or otherwise. And neither should you. Organic change? Yes. *This?* Absolutely not.'

Not after what he'd done. His dramatic exit from royal life. His brother's death.

'Your people are not ready—'

'Why wouldn't they be ready? The changes I suggest will bring my country in line with yours. Wouldn't they be more worried if we—*I,*' she corrected, 'didn't align my people with yours? The changes I want have nothing to do with your people. They already have everything I want for my people.'

'Your people would be frightened. An overhaul of everything they know overnight? Breaking centuries-old traditions?' He shook his head. 'No.'

'My speech is a declaration for positive change. The reasons for our countries merging—for *this marriage*—benefit everyone.'

He paced too. Matching her steps. Both prowling.

'You cannot wade into the royal spotlight with your dramatic sentiments and destroy the calm our marriage has brought to *my* people. If you give your little speech, it will destroy my plan for returning my country to stability. We will appear unstable.'

'*Are* you unstable?'

Natalia was perceptive.

'Our economic infrastructure is just about standing up from its knees,' he confessed, telling her what the world did not know. 'Dramatic change can be catastrophic, and for the sake of your own people, and ultimately mine, you must be gentler. Take your time. Because too much freedom, too soon, can be harmful.'

Her pacing resumed. 'Why would it be harmful?'

'Camalò is unstable in more ways than economically,' he continued. 'My brother's death snatched away everything my people believed in twelve months ago. I will not extend their pain, nor their uncertainty over their future.'

'Your brother *died*?' Her eyes searched his. Her rosebud mouth parted…inhaling, exhaling. 'I'm so sorry.'

His gut flipped. 'What game is this?'

'Game?'

'To pretend you didn't know…'

'I *didn't* know,' she said. 'Why would I?'

'You are a royal princess. Your country is Camalò's neighbour. You were promised to him—'

'I'm not kept abreast of royal deaths,' she interrupted softly. 'My knowledge of your family has been limited to the undeniable fact that I would marry Camalò's King. I *have* married him. The rest is…*was*…unimportant.'

His chest tight, he said, 'Unimportant?'

Her lips pinched. 'I'm sorry if that's a truth that hurts you. I can only imagine how I would feel, had someone said the same to me about my mother's death. But unfortunately it's the truth. I... They... My father,' she corrected, 'wouldn't have thought it important to tell me unless his death changed the facts. My father didn't even think it was important for me to know your name.' She shook her head. 'But nothing had changed. The King isn't dead,' she said softly. *Too softly.* 'He's right in front of me.'

She didn't know it was never meant to be *him*. That he was never meant to marry her.

And did it matter? Not to her. To her, she had married a king. And a king was all she'd been promised.

And there was the truth of it. She did not need him. It was not the man she was asking for help, but the King. She wouldn't have cared—she *didn't* care—which king she married, only that he was the King. The King who could help her. Not the man who'd wanted to claim her three years ago.

'He is,' he agreed, and the weight of her words and his confirmation sat heavily on his shoulders. He was King to his people and now to hers. He would not balk under the weight.

'I *am* the King,' he reminded her. Reminded himself. 'It's my responsibility alone to soothe my people and to align yours with mine. *My* way, Principessa. In time,' he said, 'your people will have everything mine do. I would not begrudge your people what my people already have,' he assured her again. 'But we will follow the path already set in motion.'

He had every intention of bringing her little nation to prosperity as he dragged his own back into the privilege they were renowned for.

'Then show me how to guide my people,' she said,

palms outstretched. 'Teach me how to be the Queen I
know I can be. Help me.'

'No,' he said. His insides seemed to snake around
his lungs. Her request hurt—like a crunching pain in
his solar plexus.

This is your chance for redemption, perhaps.

No, there was no redemption to be found here.

Not with her.

She walked to a side table by the shuttered windows.
She pulled the curtain across, revealed the night's sky
and the dim lights of the kingdom below.

She looked at the view, and he looked at her, the rapid
rise and fall of her shoulders. She stroked her fingers
across the table idly, until her hand met the lamp. The
oil lamp that—

'Don't touch that,' he warned, his insides twisting
again as her fingers touched it. The antique gold stem,
the glass housing.

It was a replica of his mother's lamp. The only personal item that had not been hidden away when she'd
simply vanished one day. When Luciano found it, his
father had taken it from him and smashed it against
the wall.

Luciano had wailed. Bereft. And his father had
slapped him across the mouth. There had been no time
for Angelo to pretend he was his brother and take the
blow for him. So he'd watched. Listened.

'We do not cry over pretty things,' King Anton had
said. 'We make use of them and then forget about them
when their job is done. Your mother, and her things, are
no longer useful to us, Luciano.' Speaking only to the
heir. The only son who mattered.

Angelo couldn't help the twist of his lips. A self-mocking smile. Because if his father had not already been dead, seeing *him* as King would have killed him on the spot.

The son he hadn't bothered to recognise.

The son he had actively encouraged his twin to ignore, because the nameless 'spare' would only weaken the future King. Drain resources meant only for the heir.

His father had been as blind as Angelo, it would seem. Because they'd both failed to realise just how much Luciano had needed his brother and his support.

Later, he'd sought a replacement lamp, with the help of the palace staff. Gifted it to his brother. And then it had become something else. Something more than a memory of their mother.

Angelo and his father had both, in their own way, failed Luciano by taking the lamp from him.

Twice.

'Why not?' asked Natalia, sliding the clasp, lifting the lid. 'I have one of these at home,' she said, picking up the box of matches that had sat waiting for a time that would never come again. 'I know how to do it.'

But she didn't. His throat closed. She didn't know the rules. Only *they* knew them. Him and Luciano.

Nightly, they would light it and talk. As brothers.

Natalia lit a match, carried the flame nearer to ignite the ready wick.

He forced his feet to move towards her. His hand reached out, grasped her wrist—

But it was too late.

The flame was lit.

And the ghosts in the room were very much alive and rising to stand between them.

'I told you not to light it.'

'But it works.'

His fingers tightened around her wrist. A heat lodged in his chest. And it spread. Downwards. Sluggish and heavy, it arrowed with accurate precision to his groin.

'It's an ornament,' he bit savagely. 'Symbolic!'

'Symbolic of what?' she asked.

He resisted the urge to tell her the rules of the lamp. The rules that had once helped him to survive. Because survival was all he had been allowed.

Her fingers flexed in his grip. 'Why didn't you want me to light it?'

He looked down at where his hand remained tethered to her wrist. He yearned to release it. Willed his body to do so. To break the electricity between their flesh, singing through his body and making his mouth itch with words he did not want to speak. But he couldn't help himself. He spoke.

'Because when the flame is lit,' he said hoarsely, 'I am allowed to forget.'

'Forget what?'

She moved. Only a fraction. But she entered his space. And the warmth of her, the scent of her, washed over him, caught him, and he moved too. Until the rise and fall of their chests synced.

'What I am,' he said huskily.

And the power of the flame, of the ritual he and his brother had performed every night, crept into his veins unbidden, like a natural reflex. It gave him the ability to set aside his title. To let his thoughts, his feelings, pump inside him unrestrained.

'And what are you when the flame is lit?' she asked, oh, so innocently.

And it was the rule, wasn't it? To answer honestly.

'A man,' he growled.

And then his attraction to her reared its ugly head, and the flame would not let him lock it away. It pumped. Flowed through him in overwhelming waves of need. Of want. To touch. To taste.

Her gaze narrowed. She broke their locked gaze, and took him in. His face. His rigid shoulders. His rasping chest.

'Are you not a man, anyway?' she asked, and placed her untethered hand on his chest, as if to test to the realness of him. The manliness.

His body thrummed under the gentle pressure of her hand. A drum, loud and strong, beat in his chest. A warning that something was coming. Something he couldn't stop.

'No.' He swallowed. The heaviness of his Adam's apple was a heavy drag in his throat. 'I am a king.'

'And when the lamp is lit you aren't?' she asked, a frown appearing on her flawless skin.

'No. I am allowed to forget.'

And he was forgetting himself now. He was shutting out duty. Shutting out the past. Zoning in on the moment. On *her*.

This had to stop.

He *would* remember who he was.

'But I will not forget who I am now,' he said, because he needed it to be true.

He made his fingers unfurl around her wrist. Released the bond of his hand. But hers remained stuck on his chest.

'And who are you now?' Her fingertips pressed into him. The pressure, the heat of her, burned through his shirt. 'I can feel only flesh. Muscle. A man.' Her slender shoulders dipped. 'And a king.'

'You need to leave,' he warned, but she came closer.

'Why?' she asked.

'Because you do not understand the rules.'

He moved backwards, made a gentle attempt to remove her hand, but she moved with him.

'Leave,' he said, but the growl of command he had wanted to summon was not what he'd voiced. His command was a broken husk. A plea not to listen but to stay.

She rose on the balls of her feet, closing the distance between them. Her breasts met his chest. And he inhaled the subtle scent of her. Daffodils in spring.

'I don't want to,' she said.

It was a seductive whisper. And all he could see were her pink lips. Her perfect, unadorned mouth. Lips parting in anticipation. Inviting him to—

'Oh...'

Her husky moan feathered his lips as she closed all distance between them and pressed her mouth to his.

And he couldn't push her away. Could not heed his own warning. He couldn't speak, couldn't acknowledge the change, the charge pulsing between them with words, but with his mouth.

He tasted her. Sank his hands into her hair.

She clutched at his shirt, and he came willingly. Closer.

He pressed into her and dipped his tongue between her parted lips. He pressed his hips to hers. Let the thickness in the atmosphere, spiced with honey, claim him.

Her hands moved to his shoulders. He trembled

against the contact. Felt the gentle pressure of her fingers as he deepened the kiss, cradling her scalp and—

She pushed. Hard. He staggered back. He reached out and she slipped through his fingers. She turned her back on him. His heart raged against his ribcage.

'Natalia!'

But she was already opening the door, moving through it.

Gone.

Angelo stilled.

He would not chase her.

He closed his eyes. Tried to think. To breathe. But the scent of her, the taste of her, was all over him. Under his skin. And it was seeping deeper into his pores, into his veins, into his bloodstream.

He'd broken every silent vow.

He held the air in his lungs until it burnt. But he could still taste her. Feel her.

She'd got inside, hadn't she? She'd cracked open his armour and revealed…

He was selfish.

She'd come to him seeking freedoms he took for granted. Freedoms he hadn't considered that she'd want.

He swallowed it down. The self-loathing.

He hadn't thought at all.

What was he doing?

God help him, he was not a boy. He was a grown man. He was the King. In control.

You just lost control.

A gut-punch, straight to the ribs, landed with a clarifying blow.

He'd landed himself in this position because he

should have compromised with her. The way he should have with his brother.

Opening his eyes, he crossed the room, yanked open the door. Thomàs, his personal secretary, was waiting for him. Angelo's duty was clearer than ever. He—*they*—needed to reach a middle ground. He needed to get out ahead of this in order to stay in control.

'Take me to her,' he demanded. 'Take me to the Princess.'

CHAPTER THREE

NATALIA MOVED FASTER through the corridor, with the lights awakening with her every step overhead.

Instinct urged her to go faster, so she did. But he wasn't following her, so why was she still running?

The butterflies inside her expanded their wings inside her chest. Flapped furiously in her chest until she was breathless.

She wasn't running from *him*, and not from the kiss, she realised, but from herself. That was why she was running aimlessly, breathlessly, through corridors, through rooms—to get to the one place forbidden to her. Because she'd been told she couldn't so often, and she was tired…so very tired…of being told that.

She'd let herself give in to her own desires, her own needs, and it had been terrifying, world-altering.

Natalia halted. Looked at the grand staircase with its intricate carved stone balustrades leading to the old Queen's quarters.

A separate palace inside the palace. *Off-limits*. But here she was. Drawn to it. To the forbidden.

Just like you were drawn to him?

Heat bloomed in her cheeks.

Natalia had recognised the need to be closer to him,

hadn't she? And she hadn't been able to stop. Drawn by some invisible string, she'd stepped forward. Touched him. Had risen on the balls of her feet and pressed her lips against his. Snatched a moment...a genuine moment... for herself.

A stolen kiss. A stolen moment in time when she had been nothing more than a woman standing in front of a man.

Her heart still thumped.

He'd warned her, hadn't he? Told her to leave. Because he'd recognised it even before she had. The change. The prickle of her skin beneath his hand, on her wrist. And it had spread up her arms, into her body. It had made her limbs heavy. Shifted her mindset, her focus, to the need to get closer to the source of the heat that had been growing in her abdomen.

He'd seduced her senses with his words. And the idea of letting herself shed her crown—her responsibilities—if only for a moment, had tempted her. Seduced her. Made her *feel*.

And she had *felt*.

For the first time in her life it had not been regret, nor guilt, encouraging her to keep moving, to step forward, but *want*. An instinctual flutter in her being to have what she wanted. And it had been irresistible. The temptation to take something for herself. For the woman she'd never let herself recognise.

She was a queen-in-waiting, wasn't she? Her sole purpose was to demand change for her people. And yet his mouth, the need to feel it on hers, had been all she'd been able to see.

All she had wanted to see.

And he had kissed her back. Slipped his tongue into

her mouth. Pure euphoria had rocketed through her as he'd flicked it, smoothed it against hers, and pressed into her with his body. His hips.

The hardness of his evident arousal pressing against her stomach had pulled her out of the heated haze sheltering them in that moment of pure instinct.

Fear had gripped her shoulders as tightly as his fingers cradling her scalp.

She'd been afraid of the unknown. Of not knowing the rules. And it had made her run. *Fast.* Away from his lips. Away from the need. The *want.* From herself.

She was still afraid. Conflicted. Two hours later and here she was, still running, still examining her responses, her reactions, to a man who had shown to her nothing but indifference.

But he wasn't indifferent to her, was he?

He'd kissed her back.

Her body moved. Took a step down. Towards the place she'd been told she shouldn't go.

Why shouldn't she go inside? This was her new permanent residence. Her for ever home. She just wanted somewhere to think in a place no one would think to seek her out.

Step by step she made her way down the stairs to a door. It was old, but solid. Cold as granite. Just as Angelo had been since they'd met. Cold and impenetrable.

He hadn't wanted to marry her, had he? He'd made that clear. He hadn't wanted to have dinner with her. He had not wanted to be near her.

But he'd kissed her back. And the muscles beneath her fingers had not been cold. No. They had been shaped and defined hard heat.

She shoved at the door. The wood creaked on its

hinges and moved. Enough to let her inside at a squeeze. She didn't hesitate. She contorted her body. Right shoulder first. Sucked in her tummy and slipped through.

There were flowers *everywhere*. Sprays of rainbow colours in oversized vases positioned on each hexagonal point of a strangely shaped room. Shelves carved into the walls held smaller vases, more flowers. Vines snaked over the walls in an orchestrated frenzy that could only be by design.

It was a secret garden.

She stepped further inside and saw that the floor was an intricate display of mosaic tiles which led down into a deep hole in the floor.

A pond. Green and lush. With water lilies gliding gently over the surface and bulrushes breaking free from the water to climb up to—

She gasped. A domed glass roof showed her the stars. So many of them…sparkling for her to see.

Plant life could not be this self-sufficient, could it? It couldn't thrive without a human's care and with only one light source.

'Hiding, Princess?'

The deep drawl of his question floated through the stillness and brushed across her skin to slip inside her ears.

Her eyes snapped towards his voice. In a room made of shadows, she couldn't find him. But she could feel him. The awareness. The thump of her heart. The thickness in the air.

He appeared through an arch. A doorway?

'Or are you lost?'

'No,' she said, because she wasn't. Her eyes flicked

up to meet his and held them despite the hiccup in her chest. 'Are you?'

'I know exactly where I am,' he said. 'And you shouldn't be in here.'

'Why not?' she countered, refusing to be cowed in her own home, however new it was to her.

She was misplacing her feelings. Zoning in on the fact that the first words he'd said to her had nothing to do with what they'd done upstairs.

And she wasn't sure if it was regret or relief she felt.

'What is this place?' she asked. Because if he could ignore it, so could she. But she pulsed with the memory of his lips.

He stepped further into the room. Towards her. 'It's a converted bath house.'

'Why would the Queen convert it?'

'She didn't need it any more,' he answered vaguely.

'Why not?' She hooked a brow. 'Didn't she like her beauty regime either?'

'It was built for her to ready herself for the King,' he answered. 'After she'd given birth to my brother and I her duty was done.'

'I don't understand...' she said.

His gaze narrowed, and he watched her for a beat too long. Until the silence felt too heavy. But she didn't let herself fill it. *Couldn't.* Her throat was too dry. Her body felt too awkward under his intense stare.

'She had it converted as a declaration.'

'A declaration to who?' she asked.

His bearded jaw tightened. 'To my father.'

'And what was your father meant to understand from her destruction of a perfectly beautiful bath house?'

She imagined it had once been beautiful. A room designed for the beautification of one woman. But wasn't it beautiful now? Changed, but still beautiful. A snippet of life inside a room where it didn't belong.

'Her duty was done, and she wanted my father to know it,' he said. 'She would never be prepared to go to the King's bed again.'

Her blush deepened with his mention of a bed. Her mind conjured indecent images of naked people being in a bed out of duty. *Them* being in a bed together...

'What happened to her?'

'She left.'

'She died?'

He shrugged. 'Maybe.'

Her eyes widened. 'You don't know?'

'I don't care to know,' he dismissed, without missing a beat.

'If you don't care, why do you keep everything alive in here?'

'I don't,' he said. 'It takes care of itself. The pond waters the plants. The dome gives them sun. They need little from me. It is an intricate design of self-sufficiency.'

'But you come here?'

'Not if I can help it.'

'That's why you closed off this wing? Why you didn't pass the Queen's quarters on to me? Because they still remind you of your mother?'

'This place reminds me of many things,' he said. 'Too many to haunt you with.'

'I don't think it's haunted,' she said. 'I think it's beautiful.'

'Do you like pretty things, Principessa?'

'Everybody likes pretty things, don't they?'

'Some more than most,' he said. 'And sometimes the

need to touch something beautiful can be a hard temptation to resist. It becomes instinctual. The primitive instinct to explore. To possess.'

He thought she was beautiful. Was that what he was trying to tell her?

A trembling took root in her core. 'Is that why you kissed me back?'

'I shouldn't have returned your kiss.' A pulse flickered in his cheek. 'For that I am—'

'Please, don't apologise,' she said.

Because she wasn't sure if she wanted to have this conversation with him. Was not sure why she'd brought the conversation back to it when she hadn't had time to figure out the reasons she'd run away when her stolen kiss had become something more. Something shared.

But she wouldn't let him shoulder the blame. It had not been his fault. It had been hers.

'I kissed you,' she whispered. 'You have nothing to be sorry—'

'I should never have kissed you back,' he rasped. 'For that I *am* sorry,' he said, ignoring her plea.

It hurt a little, but she couldn't place the feeling. She didn't understand it. But it came from somewhere deep inside her. She felt it deep in her core. And she recognised it as a woman. Not as a princess or a queen. But as a woman standing before a man…

'You came to me asking for help,' he continued, 'and I have a duty to consider your request. I should have considered your feelings long before you came to my study. You've been in the palace for two months. I have provided staff. I have provided nourishment for your body. But not for your mind. I have failed in my duty to you. Failed to provide for *all* your needs. But I have considered your requests and I will help you.'

'Help me?' she said huskily. Her heart was racing. 'Why? You were so adamant—'

'The "why" doesn't matter—only that it is the right thing to do for your people. I will help you rewrite your coronation speech. I will give you concrete plans for change to strengthen it. I will help you show them the Queen you will become.'

'And what's the catch?'

'There is none. Change is inevitable. But the pace must be slow. It will be—'

'At *your* pace?'

'No. At *their* pace,' he corrected.

'Thank you,' she said, and she meant it.

But she didn't feel lighter. Or cooler. Her skin still prickled. Her mouth still pulsed.

She bit at her lip, hard, trying to stop the words she wanted to speak because she didn't trust them.

All her life she'd waited for someone to give her the okay. Say yes to her wishes. Her plans. Now he had. In the blink of an eye, and after a stolen kiss, he'd changed his mind.

But she wanted something else…

She wanted to kiss him again. But how did she separate the very personal want for a kiss from her duty as Queen?

'Upstairs…' Her chest tightened. 'You said that when you lit the lamp you forgot who you were—your duty.'

His gaze darkened. 'I did.'

She wanted something, didn't she? Not for her people, not for duty, but for herself.

'I have one more request.'

A deep furrow appeared between his brows. 'What is it?'

She moved. Straightened her spine and made her feet move. Ignored the spike of heat flushing her skin. She didn't allow herself to focus on the tremble in her core, or the short pants of breath barely feeding her lungs. Because it made sense.

She wanted a place to hide, to reflect, to feel all the things she'd never allowed herself to feel, to be, with another person. His mother had found it in these very rooms. He'd found it with a lamp. She wanted to find such a place.

She wanted a place to examine these very feminine feelings that had made her take flight. Because she didn't want to run from them any more. These sharp currents flowing between them beneath the night sky… she wanted to hold on to them with both hands. Feel the burn. Escape into it. Understand it.

Natalia closed the distance between them until she was standing right in front of him.

This time she would be ready.

This time she wouldn't push him away.

'I want you to light that lamp with me,' she said huskily, her skin burning.

'For what purpose?'

His gaze—dark, intense—narrowed in on hers and she forced herself to tell him. To be as honest as she had with her stolen kiss. A natural response to the chemistry between them.

'So you can kiss me.'

Her body tensed. She waited for the impact of his answer to her first ever request for something for *herself.*

'Kiss you?' he growled.

And her lungs refused to inhale as she felt his rejection even before she heard it.

'The kiss was a mistake,' he said, clarifying his denial.

She'd been denied by the King and the man.

'You don't want to kiss me?' she asked, her delicate features tight in consternation. She needed to hear it. Wanted him to tell her he didn't feel it too.

'Our marriage has no place for passion.'

'Why not?' she pushed. 'I think we're allowed to kiss. Find a release from this—'

'This *what*?' He growled it from deep within his chest and it echoed inside her.

'Whatever it was that made me kiss you.'

She searched his gaze. It was empty. Dark. Nothing in there to be seen. But she could feel it. A connection she'd never shared with another human being. She'd never been intimate like this. Without words. Without acknowledgement. She knew it was there. Between them, demanding recognition.

'Whatever made *you* kiss me back.'

'I will not kiss you again,' he said. 'You want to be reckless.'

Did she?

'I don't want to be reckless,' she said, because she didn't. 'I want—'

'You don't understand what you want,' he interjected. 'You don't understand what lighting the lamp would mean. You don't *know* what it means to forget who you are.'

She recoiled. 'I'm not completely naive,' she said. But maybe she was. Wasn't that the point of her request? She wanted to understand their connection… harness it.

A stuttering breath left her parted lips. 'Tell me why not?' she asked. 'Explain your derision at extending our marriage to include kissing. Can't you feel it?' She waved her elegant hands in the air. Her fingers splayed, waving through the invisible mist. 'This heaviness?'

'There is no room in the royal world for passion, needs or love.'

'I never said love,' she corrected. 'I know love has no place in our marriage.'

Love? What did she know of it? That it hurt. That it destroyed.

'Our duty is all that can matter. I don't want your love,' she said hoarsely.

Love had put her in a cage. Love had killed her mother and put her father into a state of the living dead.

'Good,' he said. 'Because I'll never give it to you.'

She nodded. Relieved.

'At home I was a prisoner because of love,' she said.

Because she wanted him to know. To understand that she would never change her mind. That her request for them to kiss would never be about anything other than kissing.

'Love made my father afraid to live. Afraid to let his only daughter live freely without his strong arms for protection. He loved my mother desperately. To distraction.'

He hooked a brow. 'Are you asking me to give you a distraction away from your duty, Princess?'

'No.' She shook her head. 'What I'm asking for isn't the same. It could never be what my parents shared, because I do not want…*that.*'

And she didn't. But this wasn't love. It was something new. Something different. She loved her father. She knew familial love. And she'd witnessed the love that had broken her father apart. But this was like nothing she had felt before…

'"That"?' he asked.

'Love. I don't want it,' she said again.

She was making it clear. Making it known that this was not love. Would never *be* love. And he knew it too—recognised it. Because he'd said it was something primal, instinctive.

'Love made my father blind to everything but my mother, and when she was snatched away from him his world collapsed. I never want a marriage like that. So desperate. So consuming. What I want isn't love. That isn't what I feel.' She met his gaze, held it. 'Love isn't what *we* feel.'

'Then what is it?' he growled. 'What is it you think *"we"* feel, Princess?'

'Attraction, isn't it?' she said. 'And I want to explore *that*.' She swallowed, readying her throat, her voice, for her biggest confession. 'With you.'

Angelo's heart raged so fiercely in his chest he was sure it would break free of his body.

He swallowed down the temptation to reach out and pull her to him. To show her how well he could kiss. How deeply…

She's yours. She belongs—

To the crown.

'You made me realise something tonight…' she said, then trailed off.

And by God he wanted to demand she speak. Finish her sentence. Tell him what he'd made her realise.

He couldn't help himself. He asked, 'What?'

'I've never allowed myself to do anything for my pleasure. That's why I pulled away from you. I've always concentrated so hard on my duty. I've never stopped to let myself do something for the fun of it.'

'Fun?' he croaked.

A hint of a smile played on her lips, 'I think kissing you could be fun.'

She wants you too.

'It would be anything but fun,' he said, because he knew it would break him. Split his armour in two. And he knew it would never fit the same again.

'But it would be something for *me*,' she said. Her voice was low. Adamant in her conviction. 'Something *I* want. Mine. Like your mother had. Like you had with the lamp.'

'No,' he said, and watched her shoulders deflate.

The atmosphere was too charged. His mind was losing its determination to keep saying no to what his body was demanding he take.

She wanted him. Without strings. Without attachment. Without love. Only a kiss.

She was dangerous.

To his resolve.

To his silent vows.

It was dangerous to linger here in the dark. Alone. With her.

'We are leaving.' He was finished. This needed to end before his body did what it had done before. Surrendered without his permission. *'Now.'*

He turned his back on her, made his way to the arch, to the stairwell.

'This way, Princess,' he called over his shoulder.

Her footfall was light behind him. But she was following him. Up the staircase and into the rooms that had been his mother's.

He could *feel* her presence.

'Why is nothing covered if this wing if isn't in use?'

'Because it isn't,' he answered vaguely, without looking back at her.

He kept his eyes forward, but his body felt the movement of her behind him. The soft hush of her breathing.

'I understand,' she said, breaking the lull. 'I have ghosts too.'

In a room full of ghosts, he did not want to continue this conversation. So he didn't ask her what she meant. Didn't want her to ask him about his ghosts. He didn't speak. Didn't give life to the memories of the past, and the reasons why the choice had been made to turn this wing into a museum.

Because placing white dust sheets over the furniture his mother had chosen would have made it as if that time had never happened at all. A time before duty had divided him and Luciano.

His mother had chosen it all. The chaise longue to his left, with its highly polished side table made to match the intricate engraving in the loop and curl of the wood in the headrest. The gilded oversized mirror to his right. The cream and gold leaf sofas, facing one another. The cushions plumped without mercy to look as if no one had ever sat on them.

No evidence now of twins with sticky fingers... of two boys sitting right over there with their mother.

Reading them a story before their father had put a stop to their innocent gathering. Stories were for the feeble-minded, he'd said. A prince must devote his time to learning how to be a king.

They'd been four years old.

Angelo had learnt to read before Luciano. He'd become their storyteller. Hidden them away in a cupboard, behind a curtain. Read them stories of dashing knights and fair maidens.

When was the last time he'd read a book? Taken a moment to stay inside someone else's imaginative world?

Not since—

Natalia.

What would have been the point? His imagination had run riot over a woman he did not know. A stranger who had touched him more intimately than any other by simply being exposed to him.

He stepped through an open door into another lounge and turned left to open a door. He walked through it without pausing. He wanted out of this wing. Needed his present and his past far away from each other.

He was not four years old. He had no time for stories. No time for her passionate pleas for release and his imagination telling him exactly how he could do it.

She stepped through the doorway to join him. Her scent engulfed him like daffodils in spring. He closed his nostrils. Refused to inhale. Closed off his airways.

'If you make your way down this corridor, at the end there will be a door which will lead to your rooms.'

'Aren't you coming too?'

He would not walk her to her quarters.

He would not deliver her to her bed.

Because if he did, and if she invited him inside, would he be strong enough to walk away?

He did not want to take that test.

He didn't want to know how easily he could fail—forget himself and his duty again—because of *her*.

He reached for the open door. Closed it behind them. Kept his eyes on his hand, grasping the round knob.

'Goodnight, Natalia.'

She didn't move. Didn't speak.

He rose, all six feet plus of him looming over her five foot six. Her eyes narrowed. And he almost heard the question in her eyes. The demand that he reconsider.

He wouldn't.

And he needed to stamp home what she could expect going forward: his help would be limited.

'I will fix your speech,' he said, because that was what he'd promised. 'And tomorrow it will be delivered to you.'

He turned, his back flat against the door, giving her the space to move. To leave. To understand that he wouldn't follow and she shouldn't seek him out again.

Her mouth compressed. Her small body was a long, tight line of tension.

'Until tomorrow,' he said, prompting her to do the polite thing and leave, even though everything in him wanted to pull her to him. Dip his head and claim her mouth. Claim her body against the wall, the floor—

'Goodnight, Angelo,' she said, and broke eye contact.

His exhalation was deep and low, and it hurt to release it. To release her into the night without him.

He closed his eyes. Counted to ten. Waited for the click of the door behind her. For the silence. For the electricity in the air, in his veins, to dissipate.

Click.

But it didn't disappear. He still throbbed.

She was gone.

Two times in one night he'd let her go.

And his body hated him for it.

The pulse of desire was still strong. Even now, he hurt. Physically.

Then ease the pain.

Never.

His breath caught.

The past was too alive, too close.

He would not make the same mistakes again.

This was the right choice. To keep her at arm's length. Then he would never let her down. Never betray her or abandon her or disillusion her in her innocent view of the world.

He was guilty of many things, but he would not drag her into his debauched mind. Would not show her just what a depraved world it could be.

How depraved he was.

He moved. Travelled through the long, winding corridors on autopilot, his surroundings a blur, but his destination flashing in neon lights.

Far away from her.

CHAPTER FOUR

TOMORROW HAD NEVER ARRIVED.

All week he'd avoided her. The speech had been delivered the next day by Angelo's secretary. With no notes. No other messages to deliver. And the lack of any accompanying note was a message in itself. To be content...happy with what he'd given her.

But Natalia was not content. Nor was she happy.

And she had no intention of reading this speech.

The new edition was full of all the correct words. Words like 'strength', 'growth', 'building on the foundations already in place *in time*'. Simple sentences. Some short. Some long. All of them written in the correct format, starting with a capital letter and ending at a full stop. But they were empty. Cold. This was a functional script to introduce herself as the new Queen. And she was nowhere in it.

The narrator drowned out her voice.

The King had erased his queen.

He hadn't consulted her or asked her if this rewrite was what she'd wanted. He'd assumed that with his kingly pen he'd written all the words perfectly. All the right words for a princess he assumed was too naive to know any better. But the words were all wrong. They were cold and emotionless. And she was not. She was here, ready to be the Queen her people needed, and today she would show them—show *him*—she wasn't going anywhere.

It was as if that night hadn't happened.

But it *had* happened.

And Natalia felt different.

Her body…her senses… Everything was…*magnified*. Intensified.

The tingle in the pit of her stomach that would not abate. The heaviness of her breasts. Her taut nipples, peaking beneath her dress.

Her coronation dress.

It was made of shimmering silver silk with intricate beaded sequins, covering her from the rounded neckline down to her toes.

A delicate silver edging embossed each seam and curled and spiked into a maze of swirls over her breasts. Her stomach. Swooped down in vertical lines against her thighs.

Natalia wore her hair in a long French braid. Her head and hair were left clear for their new adornment. Her crown.

She twisted her hips, and the cape on her back swished with the turn of her body.

She loved it. What it represented. Soft lines and hard edges. A glittering suit of armour. And she wore that armour for her people and for herself. Life would not wound her as it had her parents.

But her flesh…

It tingled.

Eyeing the woman staring back at her in the overly large gilded mirror, she smoothed her hands over her breasts, eased her fingers over her nipples and placed her palms on the flat of her stomach. She pressed down. *Firmly*.

She shut her eyes. It wasn't a pain, exactly. But an ache. A hoarse growl of hunger. Not a gurgle, but a deep whine. And it spread out and up. The chorus sang up through her torso, echoed through her limbs to bellow in a deep finale to her fingers.

And her fingers trembled.

Was she craving a dose of something sweet? A hit of sugar? A shot of glucose...?

No, she'd eaten in her room before.

She'd requested breakfast in bed so she could linger awhile in the sheets with her feelings. Her thoughts. Before the day began. Before she did her duty with *him*.

The King she shouldn't crave.

But her body *did* crave him, didn't it?

Another kiss.

A deeper kiss.

And because of it she couldn't focus. Couldn't organise her thoughts. She hadn't slept properly in a week, but the fatigue ran deeper than that.

It was a fog. A mist over her usually firm focus.

The door to her chambers opened. Her eyes swung to her unannounced visitor and her breath caught.

The King.

'Why are you here?'

The question lacked formality, lacked anything but her reaction to his abrupt entry, and it was an accusing rasp.

'Where else would I be, Princess?'

'Anywhere but here,' she muttered, her mouth and

her body betraying her. Because he shouldn't be here. In her rooms.

Hadn't he made it clear he didn't want to be in her presence? He didn't want to share any space or time with his wife, his future queen.

He didn't want her.

'And yet here I am,' he said, stepping further into the room.

She could not drag her eyes from his. From the assured confidence oozing from his body. He belonged here. His uninvited presence was wanted.

His gaze shifted. But the relief of breaking the intensity of their shared look was short-lived, because now he *really* looked. At her.

Natalia couldn't help but stand straighter. Taller. His eyes swept over every inch of her body and she felt it like a physical caress. The tingle in the pit of her stomach intensified to gather and push down between her legs. And she didn't know how to stop it. The reaction. Her response to him.

'You look beautiful,' he said.

'So do you,' she said huskily—because he did. Breathtakingly so. A black suit, black leather shoes...

She dragged her eyes up. *Slowly.* Up his calves to his thick thighs, to the intimate section between his legs...

A flush claimed her cheeks and she made her eyes move faster. Up his broad torso to his face.

He was an impeccable specimen of a man. The gold crown on his head was an embodiment not just of the King but of the powerful man beneath it.

'Ready?' He stretched out his arm. Gold diamond-encrusted cufflinks twinkled on his wrist. He flipped his hand, palm forward, and offered it to her.

Her brain was empty. She stared at him. At the hand raised between them. Inviting her to take it. Hold it. Let her hand be held by his.

'Ready for what?' she asked.

And then something happened to his mouth. A movement…a slide of his lips.

Lips she'd tasted.

She couldn't look away. Fascinated by his full lips, thinning, curling. Smiling…

What would it be like to *feel* that smile against her mouth? On her skin?

His smile deepened and her stomach spasmed.

'Have you forgotten?' he asked.

She didn't smile back. *Couldn't.*

'Forgotten what?'

'Today…' His lips slipped again. Loosened. Parted. 'Today you become Queen, Princess, and I am here to take you to your crown.'

The fog lifted. Her lungs deflated. Inflated again in quick succession. She looked down. Away. Anywhere but at *him.*

The reflection beside her zoned into view.

'Yes,' she said. 'I'm ready.'

She stepped forward. Her heeled sliver-tipped shoes demanded she keep her spine straight. Her body was steady.

She entwined her fingers in his.

She bit her lip to stem the gasp as skin met skin.

It was a *zing.* Lemon on an open wound followed by sugar on tart strawberries.

It was a delicious contradiction of tastes on her tongue, moving through her body in conflicting waves she didn't understand.

But she wanted to, didn't she?

How could he *not* feel it?

'Then it is time to meet your people.' He closed his fist, enclosed her hand tightly in his and nodded. '*Our* people,' he corrected, and pulled her into step beside him.

It was dreamlike. Beside her the King, her husband, was a support, a strength she'd never expected, and he was walking with her towards her destiny.

She'd always been alone. Even on her wedding day. But today…

Today she wasn't alone.

As they reached the end of the corridor the doors magically opened and they didn't pause. They walked straight outside into the sunshine.

And there it was. A carriage made of glass, with spiralling columns of gold, drawn by magnificent white horses as finely dressed as she was.

She was to be paraded before the people. No blacked-out windows, as there had been on her wedding day, in the state car that had brought her invisibly to the palace, to the church, to Angelo. But a glass cage.

Today, they would see Princess Natalia. She would be flaunted through the town, and back again to the church, where she would accept her crown with the King beside her. She would walk up the aisle not alone this time, but with him holding her hand.

And she didn't know how she felt about it.

The carriage door was opened and it was Angelo who guided her inside. Who took his seat beside her. And not once did he release his hold or attempt to pull away.

She looked down at their joined hands between them on the white leather seat.

United.

'Wave, Princess,' he commanded softly, and she did.

She raised her head and looked at the faces of the gathering crowds and smiled. Waved the wave of a thousand royals before her.

And for the first time in her life she felt like a queen. Ready to lead.

She saw movement in her peripheral vision and turned to see Angelo waving too. And the crowd was not only watching her—they were also watching him. *Them.*

The carriage moved. Gravel grinding beneath its golden wheels. The hand holding hers flexed and squeezed.

She looked down again at their entwined fingers on the seat between them.

He was performing this hand-holding exercise for their audience. Not for her.

Realisation crawled through her mind and fired into her brain synapses.

Yes, the Queen was making her debut today—but so were they, weren't they? A king and queen united.

'Look up, Princess.'

Her eyes shot to his. 'I am looking,' she said. Because she was. Looking at the world, at the new life that was now hers.

'Not at me,' he corrected. 'At *them.*'

But she couldn't look away. *This* was what her people needed, wasn't it? Something they had never had. Not a tug of war between her father and mother, tradition versus modernisation, but a seamless union. A monarchy in sync.

And what did *she* need? Because wasn't she, Natalia, making her debut too? The woman who had been awakened by a stolen kiss.

It was all his fault, wasn't it? This confusion over what she wanted and who she needed to be for her people.

Long fingers curled overs hers. His fingertips were applying a small amount of pressure to make his touch undeniable. And she was very aware of it. Of him. His hand. Her hand. Of the heat gathering there, between them on the seat.

But he didn't want to acknowledge either, did he? The Queen *or* the woman. Not unless he had to. Unless duty demanded that he did. Unless duty demanded he hold her hand.

Natalia still needed his help, didn't she? Even more than she'd thought. Because there was no forgetting, was there? No falling back to sleep.

She was wide awake. And she needed his help. Not only to become the Queen she wanted to be, but to help her understand the woman he'd awoken with his touch.

When they arrived at the church Angelo stepped out of the carriage first. Silently, he guided her down to take centre stage, and his strength beside her, his support, was palpable.

Together, they walked into the church. Through the crowds gathered behind a golden barrier. The King's guard observed the joyous roars of the people who were calling both their names.

Queen Natalia. King Angelo.

They walked through the gothic-style doors into the church where they had made vows neither of them had truly meant.

Did she mean them now?

Of course not. Not her vows of devotion or love. But maybe they could find a way to give those vows a different meaning. Not love, of course. But a bond of mutual respect?

Through shuttered lashes, she peeked at him. Could she make an ally of him? A mentor? A friend?

Her step faltered, but no one would have noticed but him. The man who steadied her kept the pace of their momentum to the altar, where two thrones now sat.

You have to focus.

She did. On her every footfall, toe to heel, until they met the priest and Angelo let go of her hand. She didn't see, but she felt him step back. Giving her room to stand alone. In the spotlight.

The priest said the words she knew by rote. All her life she had wanted them to invade her ears. To change her life as she knew it.

She dipped her head, claimed the crown that had been her mother's before hers. Long, golden spiked tips encrusted with every jewel imaginable encircled her ready head.

It was lighter than she remembered from when she'd sneaked into the royal vaults back home. When her father had caught her, no doubt told by a member of staff what she was doing, she'd had to put it so carefully back inside the glass cabinet that had become a shrine to her mother.

She would not be held in a cage any more.

She turned to her audience. To the dignitaries and the diplomats, the invited citizens of her country who beamed with pride in the back rows.

Natalia wished her father was here to see this. But he wasn't. He was content to stay away. To die alone in his grief. Still too afraid to see what was happening, what had been bubbling beneath his heavy hand of protection.

This was a new era and it was everything he feared—letting in everything from the world outside their borders. Bringing in things he couldn't control. Including her. The daughter he'd swathed in bubble-wrap, protected from sharp corners and hidden away from anything that might hurt her. Like all the photographs of her mother…placed in storage deep beneath the palace.

Natalia wouldn't be kept in the dark any more, and neither would her mother.

They were free.

Head high, Natalia spoke not the words she'd written, nor the speech Angelo had rewritten for her. But new words. Words she felt were the truest yet, because they came from somewhere inside her.

'I am Natalia La Morte, daughter of Vincent and Caroline La Morte, King and Queen of Vadelto—a nation that is ready…*excited*,' she emphasised, 'to join the kind and gracious people of Camalò. And *I* am excited,' she added—because she was. 'We are ready to be taught the ways of a new world.' She met Angelo's honey gaze and spoke this part to him. To the King. '*Your* world.'

His eyes blazed and so did her blood. It roared.

'Vadelto has had its borders closed for many years, but inside them—inside our gates—we are a strong people. A people ready to learn,' she said, watching him watching her.

The current between them was strong. Pulsing with the secret wants she was exposing to him. And she felt it. She knew he understood.

She turned her gaze back to the people. 'And together—' she swallowed '—together we will stand tallest. *Strongest.* A team. Because, united, we will become strength personified.'

The applause was deafening.

She moved with Angelo towards the thrones. She took her throne as he did his, and this time she reached for his hand. And he let her claim it. Hold it.

The applause continued. *Rapturous.* And the joy in her heart was indescribable—until a flick of guilt reminded her of the words she'd forgotten to say.

A life for a life. Her mother's goals. Her mother's dreams fulfilled. Change!

She'd said none of that.

Her fingers flexed in his, but his instantly closed tighter.

She'd said exactly what needed to be said, hadn't she?

They could be a team if he let them be. And together they would put an end to whatever was burning between them.

If they worked together for the benefit of their people.

For duty.

If he taught her how…

CHAPTER FIVE

HER SPEECH HAD distracted Angelo for the entire intimate meal.

It was a small gathering of some of the heads of state
beyond their borders, and other select members of the
elite, chosen so they could nod their heads and wag their
tongues accordingly. Tell all who mattered that they had
been invited into the palace. Into the great banqueting
hall to embrace Camalò's new queen.

But he'd been oblivious to the wagging tongues on
either side of him, hadn't he?

His heart thudded painfully in his chest. Because he
had felt as if he was back in the tower, looking down at
a woman waiting to be seen. To be heard. To be summoned.

And in that church, as the priest had placed the
crown on her head, she had made herself seen.

And, by God, he had seen her.

Heard her.

Her words lingered in his ears, repeating themselves.

The declaration that she wanted what he had once
been to his brother. A guide. A support system as she
stepped into the royal spotlight and carried her people
with her on her slender shoulders.

And she believed what Luciano had, didn't she? That together they were strength personified. Because he would take the bulk of the weight for her. Carry her aspirations, her dreams, and combine them with his own.

He couldn't do it. Wouldn't pretend they could be anything other than what it had all been before. *A lie.*

His brother and he had never been strong because under the surface—under the facade of two brothers identical in skin, in flesh—they had never been united. They had been different people, with different needs and very different agendas.

Angelo had ripped at the seams which had joined them and they'd torn so easily. He'd exposed himself. He had been weak. The weaker twin all along. He'd dropped his share of the load. And the weight of the extra burden had crushed his twin...

Never again would Angelo pretend to be anything other than what he was. He would lead, he would conquer, but on his own. *His* way. No joint dreams, no facade—only what they were.

Divided wearers of the crown.

Natalia sat at the head of the long, rectangular table. Far away from him, but opposite him. She'd sat there since they'd entered the banqueting hall and been served a meal of a thousand plates.

The meal was officially ending now. Plates had been cleared. The low hum of voices, of conversations in which he'd grunted his responses to unheard questions, was winding down.

Her eyes caught his across the table...across the divide of the faces on either side. Faces he couldn't see because he could only see *her.*

Someone in the modern string orchestra seated on

a raised dais swiped a chord on a violin. A long whine.
And he felt it. The moan. Because his insides were pin-
ing. Yearning for—

He gritted his teeth.

He had stolen his brother's life, and here he was
wanting...when wanting had hurt those he had loved.

The only man he had ever loved was dead, and still
he could not let go of his greedy thoughts of having
more.

Having *her*.

It was time to end this spectacle.

He stood, and in her dress made of a thousand stars
she stood too. Elegant. Poised.

His lips parted, ready to thank and dismiss in his
regal voice, but it was she who spoke first. Thanking
them all and dismissing them with the grace of a queen.

The meal was over.

Natalia moved, and he braced himself for the scent
of her. In a swish of sliver against pale skin she came
to him. Stood before him. All at once she was everywhere. In his sight. In his nostrils, with the subtle scent
of flowers in spring. In his veins.

'Your Majesty,' she acknowledged, and then dipped
her adorned head.

It pulled him back into the room. Away from the past.
Away from his selfish needs. And it reminded him of
who he was. Who was standing in front of her.

The King.

'Queen Natalia.' He, too, acknowledged who they
were, who they needed to be in this room full of watch-
ful eyes.

He nodded to any who cared to see and offered her
his arm.

And waited.

Readied himself for her fingers. For her touch on him. On muscles rigid with painful anticipation.

Her touch feather-light, her fingers crept between his arm and his body and held on. Held on to him. And whatever was caged inside him broke free, rising to the surface of his skin with heat.

'Shall we?' she asked, her eyes hooded, sparkling.

She felt it too.

This fever.

Should they? Should *he*? He could, couldn't he? Guide her out of the banqueting hall? Show her how to remove her crown and forget her duty? Strip her to her skin and teach her the pleasures of the flesh?

Lust thrummed through him.

The battle between duty and need created an unwanted haze between his ears.

His forbidden queen was a dangerous distraction.

He would not allow it.

Couldn't.

He moved, turning his back on his people, and guided her to the exit.

And that was all he would do.

He pulled her into step beside him and they left through the doors, out to the grand hall and into a corridor full of low-lit burning candles.

'They all loved you,' he said.

It was a conscious slip of the tongue to draw his thoughts away from what he *could* say. How he could, with a few select words, clearly and undeniably acknowledge her speech and deny her.

His heart cinched. They had loved her—*did* love her—and why should he not tell her? Why should she

not have their love when she would be given no other?
He would never give her *his* love. But his admiration…?
He would not deny her that.

'Your coronation was a success. As are you, Princess,' he continued—because she was.

She had been magnificent. She'd held and captured
everyone's attention with a grace he could only admire.
A natural queen.

'Thank you.'

'You did it all on your own,' he said. 'No thanks required.'

And there wasn't. Because he had done nothing but
what duty dictated.

Angelo moved faster. Because the quicker he got her
to where she needed to be, the quicker he could leave.

He turned right. Another corridor. A long oak floor
lined with Persian rugs.

She stopped, pulling her hand free from his elbow,
and he had no choice but to stop too. Turn, face her, and
look down into her green eyes.

'Why have you stopped?'

Her eyes widened. 'I need to speak with you.'

'Then speak.'

Her hands clasped together at her midriff. 'I wanted
to say thank you.'

'You have already said thank you, and I have already
explained, Princess, that I have done nothing which re-
quires gratitude.'

'I'm not a princess any more,' she said, her slender
fingers knotted. 'I'm Queen. And the *Queen* would like
to thank the King properly for being by her side today
and for remaining there.'

'My presence was required.' His heart pumped.

Hard. 'It was not—*is* not—a gift for you, because my place will always be with my people.'

'And yet here you still are, with your people nowhere in sight.' The gentle flick of her tongue moistened her lips. 'Because it's not only your people you have a duty to, is it?'

'Is it not, Princess?' he asked, his eyes locked on to her mouth.

Her tongue had disappeared, and he wanted to tempt it back out. Seduce the soft muscle into his own mouth and suck.

He was wicked, wasn't he? Despite his vows of obedience to nothing but duty, he could not run away from what he was. From what lived inside him.

'No,' she said.

He made himself raise his gaze to hers. And remain there.

'That's why you're still here, isn't it?' she said. 'You're walking with me when there is no one to see you perform the task because you have a duty to me, too.'

'We had a duty to leave together,' he corrected. 'And we are leaving.'

He reached for her, for her hand, but she held it up, palm forward.

'And how far are you going to take me?' she asked. 'To the bottom of the stairs? Up the stairs? Or are you going to walk me to the lift, press the button, push me inside and send me on my way?'

'None of those things,' he said, not allowing himself to fall into whatever trap this was. 'We will separate at this end of this corridor.'

He pointed to the end of the vast runway of oak floor

lined with silk rugs, with a dozen chandeliers lighting the way in a softened amber glow.

'I will go to my rooms and you to yours,' he finished.

Because that was what would happen.

The only scenario he could allow.

'So many ways to get to the same destination, aren't there?'

She hooked a beautifully arched brow. So full. So defined. His fingers itched to smooth it. To ruffle the perfection.

'So many, Princess,' he agreed.

'But the only time you will come to me or hold my hand is when duty demands that you do?'

'Why ask when you already know the answer?'

'Because I'm confused.'

'About what?' His jaw clenched. His teeth were aching from the deep-set lock of his teeth.

'Why did you come to my rooms this morning?' she asked. 'Why did you take my hand? Guide me on the way when staff could have taken me to the carriage?'

'Because it was the right thing to do. Duty expected me to guide my princess to the altar to claim her crown. And I did my duty. Followed the rules and held—'

He looked down at her hands.

Her small, soft hands…

They had been so warm in his. So delicate. Their weight immeasurable because her hands had been weightless, but the impact—her skin on his, palm to palm—would remain scorched into his memory.

'I held your hand until duty demanded I step aside and release it,' he declared. Because that was the truth, wasn't it?

'Then why let me take your hand?' she asked. 'Why did you let me hold it?'

Why had he?

Angelo's brow furrowed. Tightly. And it took every inch of his control to will his body to smooth it out. To loosen his jaw. To relax the tension in his bunched biceps.

'Because you wanted to,' he growled honestly.

Almost completely truthful. Because the bit he'd left unsaid in his throat was that he had wanted her to hold it, hadn't he?

He swallowed it down...*that* unwelcome piece of honesty.

'I could hardly refuse you in front of our guests,' he hissed, like a snake warning its prey the bite was imminent.

'But you could have,' she goaded him. 'You could have refused me.'

Oh, that blush. The heightened pink tinge to her high cheekbones deepened.

'But you wanted me to do it, didn't you?' she asked. 'Because you want m—'

'You are confused,' he announced, in agreement with her earlier statement, cutting her off before she could tell him that he wanted her. Put the words in to the air and torture him. 'You have misunderstood a simple facade,' he continued, redirecting her, 'as being something deeper. There is nothing *deep* between us.'

'Did you hear any of my speech?'

'Every word,' he said, and braced himself.

How could he push her away tactfully...gently?

Because *still* she pursued him, didn't she? She kept coming back.

All week he'd kept away, to show her that nothing had changed after their kiss—after her request in the bath house—because nothing had.

He'd got himself under control. Prepared himself for today. For the impact of her. And yet still she was getting under his skin. Getting in his ears, speaking words he hadn't approved. *Didn't* approve. And he wasn't sure how much longer he could deny her…deny himself.

'And?' she pushed. 'What did you make of it?'

'It was not the speech you showed to me, nor the one I rewrote and approved. We had an understanding,' he reminded her, 'but you chose not to use the help I provided.'

'You rewrote my speech *for* me—not *with* me.'

'And you didn't use it.'

'Because it wasn't right.'

'And you think the words you rambled off to a few figureheads, a few monarchs, dignitaries and a select group of pedestrians, were the right ones?'

She tilted her chin. 'Yes.'

'You may have changed your speech, spoken your own words to my people and to me…' He leaned in and down. Until their mouths were a hair's breadth away from each other. 'But nothing has changed. I am not a teacher,' he continued. His voice rough…deep. 'I am the King.'

The burn in his gut demanded he lean in, close the gap between their lips and claim the mouth speaking nonsense. Silence her. But she was the one who moved in. Only a fraction. Exposing her throat a little more with a defiant thrust of her chest.

'And I am the Queen.'

His lips battled to remain indifferent to the sneer

building inside his muscles. But it was there. In his mouth. Set inside his jaw.

'You ignored my advice today and I shall not give it again. You are naive. *Innocent.* We are not a team. We are not united. Your speech—your expectations—are unrealistic nonsense,' he said roughly. More roughly than he'd intended.

'How can it be nonsense?' she asked softly. *Too softly.* 'The moment we stepped outside this morning, I realised the people weren't watching me.'

'Then who were they watching?'

'Us.'

'You are naive to think there is an "us", Queen Natalia,' he said, and her words from the church boomed in his ears. Words he refused to linger on any more, because they had been an innocent's view of the future. An unrealistic expectation of what he could offer her. Tutelage.

'But there is,' she corrected. 'How can there not be?' Her eyes flashed fire. *'We* are the change, we are a team, and that is what the people need. They need *us.* A king and a queen who can discuss difficult things and find the best solution.'

'What difficulties do you need to discuss, Natalia?'

What demon was inside his mouth? Why had he asked that? He knew her difficulties because he felt them, too. He knew her answer. Knew the words she had spoken in the church. The meaning under her speech. Not only did she want his guidance for her people, she wanted it for herself.

She wanted to talk about kissing. *Again.* And Angelo found it torturous not to give in to his desire right now and thrust his tongue into her mouth. Lick her neck. Every inch of her…

'What exactly would you like to discuss?' he asked again, and raised a mocking brow. Mocking himself. Calling them both out to make them recognise how absurd this moment was. 'Out here, in a corridor, where anyone could discover us or hear our conversation.'

'What other choice do I have but to make you listen to me here? Right now? Because you were going to abandon me. *Again.* Weren't you?'

Her smooth, delicate face contorted, and he felt the squeeze in his chest. The twist of self-loathing because he'd made her feel that way. Abandoned.

Like you abandoned Luciano.

He *was* going to abandon her again. He couldn't deny it.

It was for her own good.

She needed to learn he was not her tower of support. He'd offered to be that once and his brother had toppled over without him.

If she never had his support she would never miss it. Never need it. He could never fail her.

And, really, this wasn't about *her.*

None of it.

He'd taken over his brother's life and now he had to do what was right.

For his twin.

Every choice, every sacrifice he made, was for Luciano.

'You were going to forget me,' she continued. 'Pretend I don't exist when I'm right here.'

She stepped back, away from him. And his gut

tugged, demanding he follow, close the gap, stay in her space.

Instead, he planted his feet and dismissed the pull as nothing but an instinct to assert his dominance. To show her he was immune. To her. To her scent. To her words.

'I know you feel it too,' she whispered, and yet it boomed in his ears. In his soul. 'We have to have this difficult conversation to go forward in any meaningful way.'

'You think we can be a team?' he scoffed. 'An *us*?' He shook his head. Let his eyes close. 'There is no us. There is no mentee-mentor relationship. There is *no* relationship between us.'

'But there could be,' she said, and the bars of the cage containing his control shook.

His eyes drifted open. 'Natalia…' he warned.

But he didn't know what the warning was—only knew that he didn't wish her to speak any more. He couldn't stand it. Her vulnerability. Her honesty.

And his body was telling him he knew a better way. Didn't he? To silence her with his mouth, take this moment and make it his.

Make *her* his.

'There is,' she said, her eyes ablaze. Wide and watching. '*This* is happening between us, whether or not you acknowledge it.'

'Acknowledge what?'

God help him. Why did he keep pushing her for answers he already knew!

'This heat,' she answered breathlessly. 'This impulse to touch you when I shouldn't.' Her eyes searched his, her shoulders rising and falling in quick succession. 'This urge to touch myself when…'

All the blood in his body drained and pooled in his loins.

'When what?' he pushed, unable to stop himself and his selfish need to know more. To know when and how she touched herself. What, *who*, she thought of when she did.

'When I think of you,' she confessed quietly. Huskily. 'And if I don't learn how to control it...' her face twisted into lines of consternation '...it will—'

'It will what?' he growled, a rawness to his voice.

'I'm scared,' she confessed.

His throat tightened. *'Scared?'*

'Yes.' She blew out a shuddering breath. 'I'm scared that if I don't learn how to control these...*urges*...they'll consume me.'

He wanted to dismiss her feelings as foolishness, but he knew—had felt—the burning need in her. For three years it had consumed him from the inside out.

'I need you to kiss me.'

His heart stopped beating. 'We have already talked about this.'

'No,' she said. 'You talked. You said no, without consideration. Without—'

'I am still saying no.'

'Say yes, Angelo,' she said. 'Change your mind because you want to. Because you feel it too. This... awareness.'

'You do not know what you're asking for.'

'I do,' she said. 'I know what I'm asking for for our people. They need a united team. A king and queen who write their speeches together. Make decisions together without love as a barrier to what is right for the people. We will never love each other. But physical pleasure...

Now I've tasted it—' she swallowed, the muscles in her throat constricting '—I can't forget it,' she confessed.

He barely held it in. The moan in his chest.

'Teach me,' she pleaded. 'Teach me how to—'

'To control it?'

She nodded. Quick sharp dips of her adorned head. 'Yes, *please*.'

He'd tried to control it. Stamp it down. Ignore it. But here it was. The reason for his poor choices standing right in front of him, giving him what he'd always secretly desired.

'No.'

He denied her. *Himself.* He stepped back. Away from her. Away from temptation.

'But—'

'Go to bed, Natalia.'

The sparkle in her eyes vanished. The determined thrust of her chin fell. Her shoulders slumped. Her body was powering down.

He couldn't stand it.

'Go,' he growled. 'Go *now*.'

And she did. Without a word she moved. Walked past him.

That she'd actually done as he'd told her caused him to falter. He felt the cracks in his control widening, deepening. Was he really going to let her walk away? When all she wanted was pleasure? Not love? Just sex?

But what was the alternative? If he gave in to her naive seduction…kissed her again…taught her the power of pleasure…

He would hurt her, wouldn't he?

And then she was gone.

The swish of her silver dress turned left and disappeared out of his sight.

He closed his eyes. Made his body remain still, rooted to the spot, as his mind buzzed. *Rapidly.* The urge was to call her back to him. Demand she look at him. *See* him.

The tension between them had become too much. *Too real.* She was not the Princess in the garden. She was the Queen in his palace who wanted to be in his bed. And there was nowhere to run from his exposure to the reality of her. Not the woman in his head…haunting his dreams. There were no planes to board so he could run from the depravity inside him, because she was right here, demanding he give in to what he'd run away from three years ago.

The undeniable fact that he wanted her.

But what if he gave her just a taste of his depravity? She would learn, wouldn't she? Learn the undeniable fact that she could not handle him.

He didn't allow his thoughts to linger. To stagnate. He wouldn't let doubt curdle the most obvious solution— not now it had come to him.

He moved. Flying through the corridor in long strides until he came to his study. He went inside. Grabbed the lamp, the wick, the matches she'd broken the seal on, and walked straight back out.

He felt the power he held in his hands. What it would enable him to release.

The lamp would allow him to access the man he thought he'd buried on the day of his brother's funeral. The man she had brought back to life with her inquisitive touch, her questions. If he lit the lamp with her, he would give himself permission to kiss her the way he'd wanted to since their wedding day.

Since before that day.

Angelo travelled through the long, winding halls on autopilot. His surroundings were a blur, but his destination flashed in neon lights.

Her room was in sight.

If she wanted his kiss—his touch—he would give them to her. Show her those depraved parts of himself.

He moved faster. Didn't pause.

He rapped his knuckles on the door. Hard. *Fast.* Mirroring the hammer of his heart.

This was the best way.

The only way.

She needed this, but he would take no pleasure from teaching her that he was not the man for her. He would take no glory in showing her how naive she was even to consider it.

This was for duty.

To dissuade her from pursuing him.

The door swung open.

And damn him. *Damn his hands to hell.* They itched to drop the lamp. To reach out and capture her face. Pull those lips to his.

Something heavy shifted inside him.

He clasped the lamp tighter and asked the question he'd been waiting to ask for three years.

'Would you like me to kiss you now?'

CHAPTER SIX

NATALIA HAD KNOWN it was him. The harsh rap. The immediacy of her body's response to his call. But she hadn't dared to believe that it was true. That he was *here*. But there he was. Outside her door, asking her if she still wanted what she'd told him she did minutes ago.

A kiss.

He hadn't arrived and entered with an assumption that his presence was wanted. This was not an arrogant entry without permission, as it had been this morning.

He was giving her a choice.

She'd removed her crown the minute she'd entered her chambers, but his was still on his head. But he wasn't coming to her as the King, was it? He was coming to her as a man.

As Angelo.

Her eyes locked on to his mouth and her lips parted without invitation. Without her permission.

And she ached.

'Yes,' she said. 'I want you to kiss me.'

He dragged his eyes down her front to rest on her stomach. 'You want me to ease the pain…the ache inside you?'

Heat flared in her cheeks as heat swelled in her stomach. Moved down. And it dragged on her senses. Making her tingle. *Tighten.* Press her thighs together.

It was painful, the physical ache inside her. Growing.

'How do you know it hurts?' she asked, wanting to know and understanding that she had gone too far down this path not to be honest with herself. Or with him. 'Do you hurt too?'

His brown eyes pulsed, and she felt the throb in her feminine core. In her belly. *Lower.*

'Yes,' he confessed—a raw truth.

'Does it always hurt?' she whispered, refusing to let the blush burning her flesh weaken her resolve.

'Yes.' His striking cheekbones darkened, highlighted by the sharp line of his beard. 'Desire burns brightly. *Breathlessly.* Even when you name it. Claim it. Possess it.'

He understood, didn't he? Her genuine fear that she would be consumed if she didn't—

'I don't know how to do this.' Her voice cracked, as did her insides. She could feel herself splitting in two, right here, right now, in front of him. Splitting into the Princess and the woman.

'Do what?'

'To be a queen and to let myself be this…'

'Vulnerable?' he asked. 'Honest to the person you are beneath the crown of duty?'

He knew! He understood the impossibility she faced. To be this woman wanting—*needing*—him, and yet be everything else she'd devoted her life to becoming. A queen. And they felt so very different.

'Yes,' she said. 'I feel like there are different people inside my body. Pulling me in two directions. A tug of war. Both sides are powerful. Strong in their conviction. And at any time the power struggle could tip in either direction.'

'I know how to create a divide, Princess,' he reassured her. 'A way to cut the rope.'

He got bigger. Not physically. But he was all she could see framed by the door, and all she wanted to do was reach out. Touch him.

Dropping her chin to her chest, she locked her gaze onto his hands. They were so big. The strength in them was obvious. The veins pronounced. But they held something so carefully.

The lamp.

'I can teach you ways to forget who you are.' His fingers caressed the golden stem. 'Forget who *they* need you to be,' he said.

And the words caressed her. Touched her inside. Stroked something. Brought it to life.

Her eyes flitted back to his. 'With the lamp?'

'Yes,' he agreed. 'With the lamp.'

She understood then. He was waiting for her to invite him in. To close the door behind him. To shut duty out.

And light it.

That was his gift to her.

She'd always thought her people had been sleeping with their eyes wide open, but maybe she had been asleep too. Moving towards her goal without a thought for the baggage on her back. The woman beneath the load.

What else hadn't she considered? Had she truly forgotten everything other than a promise made to her mother?

Did she even know who this woman was, trembling

before a man? Because this woman was not a princess, not a queen, but someone else.

Was he trembling too? Scared to take off his crown and be with her as a man? To explore what they both knew burnt brightly between them?

She inched towards him. Knowing instinctively what she must do. Giving him her consent without words.

Whatever her stolen kiss had ignited in her wasn't going anywhere. Had he felt it too? The knowledge that their first kiss would not been their last?

He was going to give her exactly what she'd asked for. A kiss. She only needed to reach out to him.

So she did. She raised her hands and placed them on top of his, where he held the lamp. And the touch of her skin to his sent a thousand volts through her.

'Are you going to let go, Angelo?'

Was that her voice? Husky, as if her body had just woken up. Deep breaths filled her lungs. Her airways opened wider to let this fresh scent of adventure seep inside. To flow through her veins.

She was most definitely awake now.

She was electrified.

He moved. Only a fraction, but her body moved too, of its own accord, in sync with his. Backwards into the room.

They kept their hands locked. Their gazes pinned to each other.

'I am going to let go,' he assured her.

His voice was a rasp, dragging across her skin. Her breasts turned heavy. Her nipples tightened.

'But first you must understand the rules.'

'The rules?' she asked.

'This is not the beginning of a relationship, Natalia,'

he said. 'It is a way for us both to have what we need. What we crave.'

His eyes blazed and so did her insides, turning her tongue into a dead weight in her mouth. Making speaking impossible.

But she didn't want to speak, did she?

She wanted to listen to this beautiful, powerful man giving her explicit instructions. Rules she hadn't known she needed.

Maybe he understood what she needed more than she did. Because what did she really understand? She didn't understand any of this…only knew that she wanted it. His mouth on hers.

'I will kiss you for as long as you like, as long as you need,' he continued. 'But only when the lamp burns. Until it goes out. Or until you chose to blow it out. But whenever you need to light it I will come back and do it again. Do you understand, Princess?'

She did.

The lit lamp would give her permission to forget everything. Her father. Her mother. Her sacrifices. The debt Natalia owed to her people. Everything except her own desires.

It didn't taste as bitter as she'd thought it would. The confession that she wanted something for herself. That she wanted *him*. Her husband…

'You'll be here, won't you?'

'Only when the flame burns.'

She watched in fascination as his lips formed the words. In a moment they would capture her mouth, move over hers with a skill he would teach her.

'And after that?' she asked, needing whatever was

about to happen to be clear. Black and white in her mind, so there would be no confusion.

'I'll be King.'

'And I will be Queen.'

So simple. Such a clear divide…

'In the day,' she continued, clarifying the rules for herself, 'we'll be a king and queen, supporting their people.' She wanted him to understand that *she* understood. 'But at night we will be…'

She couldn't say it…couldn't put into words what they would become at night.

'Lovers,' he finished for her.

'Lovers…' she echoed, tasting the word, testing the weight of it on her tongue.

Sex. She knew that would happen between them. But being lovers? That word had never entered her mind, and she'd never considered the definition.

She frowned. 'We will make love?'

'Not love. We will have *sex*.' He dismissed her choice of words without missing a beat.

Her frown deepened. 'I—'

'I will show you every way there is to kiss…to be kissed. Until your body knows…until you understand.'

'Understand what?'

'You are a virgin,' he said. 'I will teach you how powerful sex is. Attraction. *Desire*. But never love. I will give your body its release from the pressure of royal life with sex,' he clarified. 'A pleasure you could not possibly fathom without me.'

'Pleasure?' she repeated quietly.

The realisation boomed in her ears. She'd never taken pleasure. Had had none. Never requested it. Her life was a script of duty. Of doing the right thing.

But this felt right.

He felt right.

'So much pleasure,' he agreed. His fingers loosened their grip on the lamp, sliding against hers. 'I will teach you the power of touch. *My* touch. My fingers, my lips, my tongue…exploring you, tasting you.'

She clenched her hands, as if tightening her grip on this gift to her.

A gift she knew was more than she could understand right now.

It was an awakening.

He let go. Removed his hands. And she felt the weight. Not of the lamp. But of the choice he was giving her. To turn around. To walk inside. To light the flame. To create an illusion of freedom.

With him.

'Shall we?'

She blinked, clearing the fog, and looked at him. The King at her door. The husband who was practically a stranger, waiting for her to decide what happened next.

To make her choice. Her decision.

Was she ready for this commitment?

'Yes,' she said huskily. 'We shall.'

She dragged her eyes from his, felt the loss of his cool confidence and tried to summon her own.

She turned. And he followed.

The soft click of the door sealed them inside with nowhere to go but forward.

A heavy metallic clink on a hard surface penetrated her ears. She didn't look back. She knew what he had discarded. His crown.

Now they were both stripped of their duty, weren't they? Bare. Naked.

They were exposing themselves to each other in rooms that were much the same as the rooms in the rest of her life. As in her palace at home. Luxurious rooms of exalted opulence. No signs of the individuality of her existence. Just rooms full of fine silks and antique furniture which no price tags could be attached to. Priceless things collected by and gifted to monarchs before her time. Before his.

She had always been another 'thing' to her father. Something priceless that had to be cared for. Protected. Her thoughts. Her words. Her individuality.

Her breath caught. Her throat was too dry, her skin too sensitive. Because amidst it all, despite their royal masquerade, they were here, heading to her bedroom because she wanted to go there.

Stop thinking!

She did. She blocked it all out. Everything but the heat of the man behind her. Her trembling grip on the lamp. The whoosh of her heart…a tidal wave of excitement. She didn't slow her approach as they crossed through the lounge, came face to face with her door.

Her bedroom door.

'Wait.'

Natalia did as he commanded. Froze.

She closed her eyes, allowed herself to feel the crackle of electricity sparking between them. It skated across her skin, intensified as he drew closer. Until he was just a step behind her and the fire between them roared.

His breath hit her nape. 'Not the bedroom.'

Her eyes flew open. She tried to turn. He pressed into her. Only lightly. Just enough for her to feel the shape of his body.

She swallowed. 'Why not?'

His fingers touched her scalp, oh, so gently. Buried themselves in her hair. And she felt them move, loosen the French braid until her hair fell about her shoulders.

'Not yet.' He swiped her hair forward in front of her left shoulder, exposing the tip of her spine.

His words fanned her neck.

The heat of his breath dragged a gasp—no, a moan— from the deepest part of her. It rushed out of her mouth and made itself known in the silence.

She trembled. 'Isn't one room the same as any other?'

'No, Natalia,' he said, and cool air washed over her. The caress of his exhalation. 'It isn't. When you invite me into your bedroom…into your bed…it will because you want me there with you. To touch you beneath your clothes. To teach you the pleasures to be had with my body inside yours.'

She was so tempted to lean back. Press herself into the heat of him behind her. But he was right. She wasn't ready for him to get into bed with her. Slide in between the sheets.

Inside her.

She didn't know if she was ready for them to go further than what he'd promised. Not tonight. But she *was* ready for his kiss.

'Where should I light it?' She tilted her head as she whispered. 'The lamp?'

'By the sofa.'

Heart racing, she moved to the side table next to the maroon three-seater and placed it down. Lit it. Before she could examine the shadows dancing on the wall he was coming back to her. Reaching out. Hands so steady. So calm.

He cradled her face. He descended. And she couldn't look away. Didn't want to. Dark lashes fluttered down to shadow his impressively high cheekbones and closer he came.

Not a stolen kiss this time. Not a quick explosion of desire. But a slow promise of what was to come. What they were going to explore together.

And this time she was ready.

She closed her eyes. Braced herself for the impact of him. But his lips didn't meet her mouth. They feathered her cheek. And then the other. The light pressure of his mouth moved over her forehead, her eyes.

She trembled. A silken warmth gathered in the heart of her, pulling her thighs together.

His mouth moved again. The same feather-light kisses. His fingers tightened. Gently but firmly applying pressure at her nape to arch her neck.

He placed his mouth to the pulse throbbing in her throat and sucked.

Every nerve-ending in her body exploded under the gentle pressure of his kiss.

'Angelo—'

'Shush…' he said against her skin. And it hummed. Sang for him as he kissed her neck harder.

She knew his kiss would leave a mark. That this moment would be with her even when he wasn't. When the lamp was cold and duty burned hot.

His hand moved to cradle her scalp gently, and he sank his fingers deeper into her hair. Moved his mouth with a slow urgency up her throat.

He was holding her gaze steadily with his, his eyes black. 'I am going to kiss your mouth now,' he warned her. Readying her. A gentle instruction to prepare her lips.

She couldn't speak. She nodded. Felt his fingers flex with the dip of her chin.

He pulled her mouth onto his.

It wasn't quick and impulsive, as it had been in his study, but careful. He increased the pressure slowly. Coaxed her mouth open to accept his tongue.

His tongue sank inside her wet heat and she moaned. It was an audible admission. She was lost. Out of control. And there was nothing she could do about it but accept it. She was too enthralled with her body's response to do anything other than *feel*.

Angelo deepened his kiss. Her tongue met his, sliding against it. Instinctively, she leaned her body into his. The hardness of him pressed into her stomach.

She gasped. Her eyes flew open and so did his. He broke the kiss, and she tried to steady the rasp of her breath, the hammer of her heart.

'Enough?' he growled, and she knew he asked the question because he remembered the last time she'd felt his arousal…what she'd done.

Run.

But she wasn't afraid this time, was she?

She was enraptured.

'No.' She shook her head. Her body hurting, 'More,' she demanded.

And she kissed *him*.

Standing on tiptoe, she pushed her tongue inside his mouth and he met her show of desire with his own. Swept his tongue against hers. Encouraged her to go deeper. To kiss him as he had kissed her.

And she did. Furiously moving her mouth with a naive enthusiasm.

He broke their kiss again.

And this time she sobbed with the loss of contact. Felt the pressure in her stomach. Deep in her body.

'Natalia, sit down,' he croaked.

Her features twisted into a flushed frown. 'On the sofa?'

'Yes.'

'Why?'

His features were schooled. Unreadable.

'Do you like my tongue?' he asked.

Heat flared everywhere. On her cheeks. On her skin. Inside her. Between her thighs.

'Very much,' she confessed.

Because if she couldn't confess the truth here, when *could* she be honest?

'Would you like to feel it again?' he asked.

Her toes curled inwards. 'Yes.'

'If you sit down, I can show you another kiss.'

'Another kiss?'

'So many kisses, Princess, I will show you,' he promised.

She sat. Faced forward. Knees together. Fingers knotted in her lap. And waited.

He knelt on the floor before her and reached for her feet.

Fascinated, she watched as Angelo removed her silver shoes and discarded them on the floor with a gentle thump.

'If at any point you dislike what I am doing,' he said, making his words clear, 'and if you want me to stop…' He stroked his forefinger against the arch of her right foot. Her gaze snapped to his. 'Tell me and I will stop. Without pause. Without hesitation. Do you understand?'

'I do,' she said. 'But please don't stop.'

Why would she want him to stop this? The completely unexpected pleasure of a man playing with her feet. Her ankles. Such an innocent place for skin to meet skin. To touch. Yet it felt wicked. *Delicious*.

'I won't,' he said. 'Not unless you ask me to.'

'I won't ask,' she said. Because she wouldn't. She wanted this. Him…

'But you can,' he said again.

Her breath caught. Her heart hammered. *Her* choice. So many choices had been taken away from her. Her destiny was preordained. Her marriage an emotionless union for the sake of her people.

But this…

This was hers and hers alone.

She flicked the pink tip of her tongue over her mouth. 'Kiss me now,' she demanded. Because that was what she wanted. All she'd been able to think about. His lips on hers.

'I want to kiss you here…' He smoothed the pad of his thumb over the knot in her ankle bone. 'Can I?'

'Yes.'

He did. Feather-light. A tease of his mouth, his breath.

He raised the hem of her dress. 'I'm going to go higher, Natalia,' he warned softly, and he moved his hand over her ankle.

His mouth was moving with his hands, pressing kisses to her skin, to the plump softness of her calf, as the fabric of her dress rose higher.

And she closed her eyes. Because how could she not when her body was tightening, squeezing involuntarily?

'I'm going to kiss you here.'

She opened her eyes. Watched as the light caress of

her dress skated over her skin and exposed her legs. He laid the folded fabric to rest there. At the top of her thighs.

'Where?' she asked, unsure where his lips were targeting. But even with his touch absent she felt him everywhere. In the whoosh of her heart. In each rasping breath.

'Here,' he said, and dipped his head, pushed his mouth against the join behind her knee.

Her breathing accelerated, and he kissed her harder. Sucked. Flicked his tongue. Soothed it up and down the crease.

She squirmed.

Instinctually she tried to pull her thighs together. Tried to stem the heaviness. The urge to clench her intimate muscles tight.

He gently gripped her calves, widened them, and positioned himself between her thighs.

She shivered.

'Kiss me now, please,' she said, ready not to think at all, but *feel*.

'I am kissing you,' he said.

'Kiss my mouth,' she said. A broken sentence. Simple words. A confession of where she needed his lips.

'Not yet,' he denied her. 'I am going to kiss you slowly in all the places you have never been kissed.'

'Okay…'

'Here…'

He kissed the scar on the side of her knee. A little nick from an insignificant fall. No one had ever kissed it. Not to make it better or ease the pain. And she wasn't sure if his kiss was hurting her or making it better.

But she wanted more.

'And here,' he said, and kissed her thigh.

His lips were so soft. *So hard.* So masterful. Opening and closing with a skill that worked on her skin, her senses. Affected her breathing.

Everything in her wanted to feel those kisses everywhere. To close her eyes and give in to the whine in her stomach. The groan singing in her veins that echoed from her mouth in little gasps.

But she couldn't look away from the dark head nestled between her legs. The head now turning to give each thigh the same attention.

She was burning. On fire as he raised his head, eyes blazing. 'Can I go higher?'

There was only one place that was higher.

The pulsing heart of her.

'Please…' she pleaded. Because she needed his touch there, didn't she?

He held her eyes as his hands climbed higher. Caressing softly. Stroking. And it was as if he could hear her body screaming. She needed his touch *harder.* Because his thumbs were digging into her thighs.

And she moaned.

It was a release of pressure. A moment's reprieve before his hands moved to the high crevices of her thighs. The seams of her knickers. And stroked.

'Oh!' she gasped. *Whined.* It was a tickle. A caress. Almost painful. Delightful agony. Her intimate core clenched.

'Do you like my fingers here?' he asked.

And, yes. Oh, yes, she did.

'Yes,' she said huskily, and he stroked again. At another join of joints. And it wasn't enough. It was *too* much…

'I need…' she started brokenly. Her breath shuddered from her lips. 'I need more.'

'More?' he confirmed.

His voice was a broken husk of the need she felt. And she recognised his single word for what it was.

A promise of pleasure.

He dipped his head and she gripped the sofa beneath her fingers. Tightly.

His thumb pulled aside damp fabric and he licked her.

'Angelo!' she screamed.

Because this was an intimate kiss her books had never told her about. But she wanted it. His mouth there…on the part of her that throbbed. *Pulsed.*

And then he was lifting his head. Pulling away.

'Please, don't stop,' she begged. Because this was agony. An unknown, beautiful frenzy of pain and delight.

'I'm not going to stop. I'm going to kiss you again. At your core. I'm going to suck it. Tease it with my tongue.'

'Oh, good God…' she moaned.

His warning was too direct. *Too real.* But she'd asked for instruction and he was guiding her into the unknown pleasures to be found in her body. With his body on hers.

She'd asked for this. Begged…

'Please…' she whispered. 'Do it now,' she begged.

Before reality could creep in. Before this moment she was allowing herself was over too soon. Before she could find the release she craved and the release she knew only he could give her.

'When I kiss you again, Princess. I want you to listen to your body and do what it tells you to do.'

He curled his palm over her mound and pressed down. Cupping the heart of her in his hand.

'What if my body doesn't know what to do?'

'It will,' he rasped, 'and my kiss will guide you.'

Gently, oh, so gently, he swirled his tongue. Slipped it upwards and then down again. Repeated the action before he caught the swollen nub peeking out from her dark curls between his lips and sucked.

Just as he'd promised he would.

'Oh, oh, oh!' she panted breathlessly.

His free hand moved over her arching hip, locking her in place. Holding her. Guiding her.

The hand cupping her so intimately moved. His fingers stroked her folds. Her opening.

He was right. Her body was talking to her.

She wanted to bear down on his stroking fingers. But he was sucking that nub between his lips too urgently. His fingers stroked her wetness over her folds too expertly. The intimate muscles inside her clenched. Spasmed.

And then it happened.

His fingers curled, cupped her, and applied a wonderful pressure to the growing need inside her as he sucked faster. *Harder.* And she rocked against his hand. Thrust up against his mouth.

She took flight. Getting higher and higher. The pinnacle unknown.

'Angelo!'

She screamed his name until she felt as if she was floating, boneless, weightless.

She felt free.

And then, minutes later, maybe hours, she was landing. Coming back to the man between her thighs. The man fixing her underwear. Righting her dress. Sliding the fabric down her thighs, her knees.

The whisper of his fingers skated over the oversensitive skin of her calves and his eyes locked on hers. His face was a mask of hard lines. 'Are you okay?' he asked softly, contradicting the stillness of his body. The rigidity.

Was she?

Breathless, her heart still beating abnormally she confessed, 'I don't know.'

Her voice was not her own. It belonged to the pleasure in her limbs, didn't it? Making her soft, sleepy, but alert. Still aroused…

'How can I feel like this when before—' She bit her lip.

'How *do* you feel?' he asked gently.

'I thought female orgasms were a myth,' she confessed honestly.

Because that was what it had been, wasn't it? An orgasm?

'Your books are out of date, Natalia.'

The fire in his eyes was so dark, so hot, she could *feel* it.

'An orgasm is a powerful release for both men and women. The female orgasm can be elusive to unskilled hands. But you're very sensual. *Responsive.*'

The warmth in her bones spiked.

'Was this your first orgasm?'

'Yes.'

A pulse flickered at his temple. 'And how do you feel?' he asked again.

'Relaxed,' she said, her abdomen pulling tight. 'Aroused…' She exhaled heavily.

His nostrils flared. 'I want you to touch yourself.'

She blushed. Felt the deep red embarrassing blanket on her cheeks.

'When you are alone,' he added. And his smile was tight, the colour of his irises swallowed by the black of his pupils.

'Why?'

It was the only question she could think to ask. The only word her tight, dry throat would allow.

'Because you need to understand your body better,' he said. 'Learn how to ease the ache on your own.'

'Oh…' she said.

'I won't come to you again for a week.'

'A *week*?'

'For one week I want you to touch yourself. Explore every part where it feels nice to touch. And when I come back you will tell me where you would like to be kissed—*touched*—by me.'

'I've never—'

'You're allowed to. With or without the lamp. It's your body. *You* are in charge of your pleasure. Of how many times you want to find release.'

'But…' She swallowed. 'I can find my release whenever I want?'

'Whenever you like,' he agreed.

'But this? With you—'

'Only with the lamp,' he said, reminding her of the rules. Of the flame flickering beside them.

And for the first time in her life Natalia realised she could satisfy herself. *For herself.* For no one other than herself.

'Sleep well, Natalia.'

She sat upright. Her heart pounding. 'You're leaving?'

Feather-light, he stroked her cheek. 'I am.'

'But—'

He stood, bent down and brushed his mouth against hers. Placed his open palms on her flushed cheeks and pulled her closer. His lips pressed a little harder and she softened to the pressure. Her mouth parted. Opened for the tease of his tongue.

All too quickly Angelo pulled away.

'One week,' he reminded her.

He looked at her and she looked at him.

'Goodnight,' he said, and removed himself.

From the sofa. From her touch. Turned off the lamp. Walked to the door and did not look back.

He left her behind. Still panting, aroused and afraid. Afraid that he might never return.

He'd given her what she wanted, what she'd asked for, and yet her body wanted more.

Was she so selfish?

Was she so very wrong to want him?

Because this illusion, this set-up they'd created, was too real, too much. She wanted to do it all over again. With him.

CHAPTER SEVEN

ANGELO HAD TOUCHED HIMSELF.

Every day for the last week. Every day in the shower he'd pictured her face. Her rosebud lips, her tongue sliding against his as he pushed his deeper inside her mouth.

He wanted to go to her. *Now.* Forget every vow, every rule, and imitate the kiss they had shared with the thicker, swollen length of him. Sink himself inside her. *Deeply.*

But of course he wouldn't.

Couldn't.

He gritted his teeth. He knew the rules. He'd made them. And they weren't working. He'd condemned himself to this agony in the shower, where he never eased the ache.

Physical release was easy. It was friction. But this... this wasn't physical. Because the wish lived inside him. The warm beads of water sliding down his bare back were her hands. The never-ending want whispered in his ear and demanded that her fingers bite into his shoulders, that she wrap her legs around his waist.

And he wanted so desperately to grip her soft, fleshy thighs. Part them. Allow her a moment—*a second*—to accommodate the size of him, the impact of him pressed against the core of her, and then—

Aching, he gripped the swollen length of himself in his hand. Closed his eyes. Lifted his face. Let the water crash into the tight muscles clenching his jaw, bunching his shoulders.

But he couldn't wash it away. This constant yearning for the scent of her to fill him, for the taste of her to bring his senses alive. Because she'd matched him, hadn't she? Matched him in his desire.

His lesson in depravity hadn't worked, because she'd met each stroke of his tongue in her mouth with a swipe of her own. Moaned as he'd kissed her knees, her thighs, and lifted her hips to meet his demanding mouth.

Natalia hadn't shied away from his wickedness, from his lips eliciting the increasing rasp of her breath. No. Her gasps of excitement had been unrestrained as he'd stroked her. Pushed her to understand that his demands on her body would be too much for an innocent like her.

But she had not understood. Not in the way he'd imagined she would.

She'd claimed her desire and surrendered her body to him.

And her surrender had awed him. Shocked him. Enthralled him. Watching her learn that her body could do that...that he could do that to her...he was obsessed with it.

With her.

But he'd always been obsessed with her, hadn't he? And there was no going back now. Because his every thought was clouded by her, no imagination required.

He knew her taste.

A taste so divine he would spend the rest of his life

searching for a substitute. And he knew he would never find it. Because he wanted no synthetic replica.

Hadn't he tried to find a substitute before? Before he'd experienced Natalia? The realness of her? And those brunettes' names—faces—had blurred into nothing now. They all paled into nothing because he'd had her.

He was losing sight of himself—of the rules. Because he couldn't forget what he'd instructed her to do. To touch herself the way he longed to. And when he touched himself he imagined his hands were hers and forgot the reason for his lesson. For the week's separation he'd inflicted on them both.

He'd instructed her to touch herself, to prove that she didn't need him to help her. She could ease the ache all on her own. She did not need him.

But he didn't want her to ease the ache alone.

He was a selfish bastard.

Still.

He slammed off the shower. Today, he'd showered three times. But the ache remained. *The hurt.* Because, however many times he gave himself release, he knew the truth.

He was a substitute for his brother.

If there had been a choice—if she'd had to choose—she would never have chosen *him*.

He stepped out of the shower. Wet, hard, and still aching for his queen, he got ready to face her.

He dried himself off, slipped on underwear and black silk socks. He strapped the sock braces to the bulge of his lower calf and clipped the silver buckles. He thrust his legs inside his trousers, put on his shirt, his jacket, tie and shoes…

He made his mind stay blank. Calm. Because it didn't matter how much he ached—it wasn't about him.

It had never been about him.

He combed his hair and then reached for his crown. The gold was cold beneath his fingers.

He placed it on his head. Let himself feel the weight. The heaviness of regret that he carried for his brother. He would carry it now. Wear it for his brother and carry it all.

Because only the King would stand beside her tonight.

Because that was all he could allow himself to be.

Until—

Her lips flashed in his mind. Her voice was in his ear, demanding he *Do it—do it now!* He inhaled deeply. Pushed down his greedy desire.

Tonight was the coronation ball. A celebration of them and their union. And when it was over, when his duty was done, he would kiss her again. But only then.

Angelo moved. Walked out of his chambers and headed for the grand staircase where he'd told his staff to tell her to meet him before they were introduced to the guests in the ballroom.

It had been a conscious decision. A decision to keep him out of her rooms until it was time. Until he had permission to lose his head and teach her how to lose hers. To teach her the pleasure he could give her. To teach her that he was too much, too needy, too greedy for an innocent virgin. Too selfish for his forbidden princess to tame. And that she must stay far away from him.

Heart steady, he breathed in and out, put one foot in front of the other, and walked. Through the corridors. Past the ghosts lurking in every shadowed corner.

He kept his focus on the door ahead.

On where it led.

To duty.

He didn't falter. Didn't hesitate.

He opened it, walked through—

All the air left his lungs in one deep, long exhalation. Like a drop-kick to his sternum. To his gut. Because there she stood.

Waiting for him.

She wore a backless red dress. Her shoulder blades, her spine, her skin, were exposed all the way to the slope in her lower spine. Puffs of silken lace flared at her hips to fall to her feet, and in between the lace were diamonds. Tiny little gems that sparkled.

As did she.

Natalia turned to face him.

Every inch of her was concealed. The red encircled her throat and feathered down her arms to her fingertips. And her face was a vision of sparkling golds and crimson lips…

'Natalia,' he acknowledged.

His voice was too rough. *Too raw.*

She stepped towards him and he couldn't tear his eyes away. He ignored the warning lights flashing in his mind's eye and stepped forward.

'Angelo…'

He winced internally.

Immediately he recognised his mistake. His lack of formality. Duty waited for them just through another set of doors and down a staircase of thirteen steps and he had forgotten. In the blink of an eye, he had forgotten himself. Named his queen and given her permission to name her king.

'Is everything all right?' she asked, her dark lashes spanning her eyes, so thick, so dark. 'Are you okay?'

His gut twisted.

The gold sparkling beneath her eyebrows and dotted in the corners of her green eyes gave the illusion that her eyes had no end. He would not fall into them. He would not drown in their endless depths. He would not lose his head and tell her that *No, he was not okay.*

But was it so obvious? Could she see what no one else ever had? That beneath the facade, beneath his crown, he had never been okay. Had he?

No one had ever cared if he was okay. Even when he'd laid his brother to rest, the empty casket a symbol of the end of an era, the end of his brother, no one had asked him. But here she was…asking.

'Yes,' he rasped. 'Everything is fine.' He sucked in a lungful of air. *Of her.* The scent of spring. Of flowers ready to bloom. 'Shall we?'

'We should.' She reached down and claimed his hand, entwined her fingers in his.

Dark lashes swept upwards and her eyes glistened with something he couldn't recognise. *Did not want to see.*

It slammed into his chest.

And he could not recover fast enough.

Because beneath it all he was raging, wasn't he? He was angry at it all. Angry at *her* most of all. For making him see what he was. Who he was. Three years ago, in that garden, she'd exposed him. And she was doing it again now.

Exposing him.

In those gardens he'd seen a version of himself, hadn't he? A woman—his counterpart—playing the royal waiting game. He'd built up this idea that they were the same. That they wanted more…that they wanted everything.

And none of it made sense to him. Not this nonsensical pull in his gut to get closer to her. To claim her. Because that represented everything he was and everything she wasn't.

Selfish.

'Are you ready?'

Oh, so gently she asked her question. And she remembered, didn't she? Who they had to be. Who he needed to be.

'Yes.' He nodded. A deep dip of his head. And let her guide him to double doors made of black wood and golden hinges.

The doors opened. They walked through, down the stairs, and everyone in the room stopped.

'Their Majesties King Angelo and Queen Natalia.'

Everyone turned.

Her fingers flexed in his.

And it consumed him. The awareness of her standing next to him. The realness of her. The quiet strength radiating from his queen.

Her hand was so warm in his. So delicate.

His heart pumped. His veins bulged. His brain screamed.

What if he didn't hold back the instinct tugging on his nerve-endings to hold her hand more securely? What if he leaned down and feathered his lips against hers? What would their marriage look like if she let her hand steady him as he steadied her? What if he allowed them to be a team?

He'd hurt her…

He willed himself not to hold her hand in his big palm too tightly, but despite himself…despite everything… Angelo squeezed.

Natalia had been swept and twirled into a thousand arms but not his.

A thousand different shades of colour filled the dance floor as an orchestra played a mix of contemporary ballads and traditional tunes. The clinking of glasses pinged within the hum of low voices. High-pitched laughter erupted from the tables around the great ballroom. Chandeliers flickered from the high ceilings.

But Angelo's presence shone brightly in a room full of nondescript shadows, because she had known all night without looking where he was.

Because she *felt* him.

He was something familiar in a room full of unfamiliarity.

Her eyes found and locked to his over the shoulder of the man who had claimed her hand for a dance when she'd barely let go of her previous partner. Dark eyes stretched over the distance between them and held her entranced.

Angelo was every inch a king. Surrounded by bowing heads and bent knees, people hanging on to his every word, watching every tilt of his head. But his eyes, as they had all night, remained on her.

'He can't take his eyes off you.'

'Pardon?' she asked, ripping her attention from Angelo and placing it back where it should be. On the European prime minister with two left feet.

'The King. He can't take his eyes off you.' A mouth

accentuated by lines showing a life lived, sharing many smiles, smiled at her. 'As I see neither can you take yours from him.'

She blushed. 'I apologise.'

'Please, no.' He shook his head. 'It's a joy to see young love bloom under a nation's gaze.'

Love?

She forgot her feet. The steps. Made one step forward, one to the side, followed by one backwards, another slide—and trod on his feet instead.

'I'm so sorry, my dear.'

'This time it was me.' She smiled. Too brightly. Too thinly. 'Edgar,' she added, too late, and flashed her teeth.

A deep chuckle vibrated in his upper chest and his grey combed-back hair fell forward. 'Eddie, please, Your Majesty.'

'Eddie,' she confirmed.

'Edgar makes me feel so old,' he confessed, and manoeuvred them through another waltzing couple. 'I have lived many years, and through the reigns of many kings and even more princes, but your king is a unique breed.'

She frowned. 'Breed?'

'The type of king who has had to lose it all in order to learn what being a king actually means,' he explained, explaining nothing at all. 'And those kings are usually the best ones, don't you agree?'

'Don't I agree with what?'

'Your king has lost his mother, his father and his brother. His entire family—*gone*.' He blew out a puff of air and she refrained from removing the spots of spittle from her cheek. 'And his brother was lost so tragically, of course.'

'Tragically?' she said huskily.

'My dear...' He searched her gaze with narrowed eyes. 'The fire.'

'Fire?'

He nodded. 'King Luciano—'

'*King* Luciano?' she repeated, waiting for his correction.

'Yes,' he confirmed. 'Young Luciano—such a promising king—died in a fire in the mountains. In Camalò's second palace. The fire ravaged everything. There was nothing left...no body to bury... It was whispered that we'd never see Angelo's return—'

'Where *was* he?'

'Angelo?' His eyebrows flew high. 'Somewhere on the outskirts of Europe,' he answered. 'But he came home, your king. To his rightful place with his people. And it is such a joy, brings me such peace, to see him with you after so much tragedy.'

Her brain spun.

'Your Majesty, I did not mean to upset you or speak out of turn.' His wrinkled cheeks turned scarlet. 'I am old. I speak as I find, perhaps not as I should.'

She couldn't answer.

She hadn't spared Angelo a thought, had she? She'd been so focused on what he could do for her, she hadn't even considered him. Hadn't considered him at all. She hadn't even asked Angelo how his brother had died that night in the study...

The music ended and her heart hammered. Because she knew it was him. Behind her. Her body had reacted. Tightening. Tensing.

Edgar released his hold on Natalia, stepped back and bowed deeply. 'Your Majesties...'

Angelo placed a hand on her hip, and as he came into view everything else faded. Dimmed against his brightness.

'I believe the next dance is mine,' he said.

He moved, and her body moved with him. And she didn't need to remember the steps, didn't need to tell her body which way to turn or twist, because she was weightless in his arms. Flying too high above the music to hear the notes. Only their breathing. The whoosh of her heart in her ears. The tingle of his skin against hers.

And those butterflies stormed through her. Unbidden. *Unwanted.*

Her voice flew above the surge of awareness in her chest, in her body, as she said, 'I want to talk.'

'About…?'

Her fingers tightened on his shoulder. 'Your brother.'

'He is dead.'

'He was the King, wasn't he?' she asked, her heart racing. '*He* was the man I was meant to marry.'

His eyes darkened into empty pools of nothing, but the pulse in his cheek flickered.

'And?' he asked.

'And,' she repeated, 'I didn't know.'

'You said his death was unimportant.'

'You kept me in the dark—'

'No,' he rejected. 'You kept yourself in the dark. All you had to do was ask the right questions, or embrace the internet, and you could have found out for yourself. But you didn't. You didn't want to know. Because none of it mattered to you, did it? Not the world outside your kingdom, or the death of my identical twin brother. Because they did not affect *you*.'

'Yes,' she said, trying to make sense of her feelings, her thoughts, here, now, in real time, with him. 'I wanted a king. I *needed* one. But I didn't ever know *who* I was marrying. Only that I was to marry a king. Only that he would gift me a crown. When I did receive my crown, I knew it wasn't only about me any more. It was about *us*. And now—'

'You wanted a king.' His shoulders stiffened beneath her fingers. 'Well, here I am, Princess.'

'I thought all I needed was a man with the title,' she said. 'A king. *Any* king. I didn't know it would be *you*. And the idea that it might not have been you...'

'Do you feel cheated because they gave you the spare, Princess?' He smiled. But his lips were lying. They curled and lifted in all the right directions to reveal perfect white teeth, and yet his smile was something else. *Something ugly.* 'Am I not everything you wanted your king to be?'

'I never imagined you at all,' she confessed. 'But now I can't stop thinking about you. And now...'

'And now?'

'I want to know *everything* about you.'

'There is nothing to know,' he dismissed—so easily.

'There is *everything* to know,' she countered. 'I want to know where these feelings come from. Why they are happening to me. *To us.* We have been thrown together into a marriage that should mean nothing to me—and yet it does. I want to know what your life was like before I came into it. Because you're right. I have been in the dark. Because I let myself stay there. I made myself content with the life I had because I knew that one day a king would come. *Any king.* I didn't care. I only cared that he would allow me to have the crown I needed to pay back the debt I owe to my mother. To my people.

To my father.' Her chest tightened. 'And when that day came…the day I'd thought about all my life…and it was *you*, and you kissed me…'

His eyes blazed and her stomach whined.

'You made me feel things,' she confessed. 'Question everything about myself. Who I am. And I am not content any more. Because I deserve the facts. I deserve to know *you*. I want to know. Because I care about you. Not as any king, but *my* king.'

He looked at her as if everything she was saying was wrong.

'I am *their* king.' He placed his mouth to her ear. 'I belong to the people, as do you.'

His lips were so close to her skin she could feel them. Sense their movement as he spoke.

'This is why there must be rules between us. Definitive lines. A clear divide to remind you who you are and who I am in this room.'

'And who are we?' she asked. Because he'd made the rules. Set out his conditions. But her body wasn't listening. It didn't care. It only wanted to be here. In his arms. Feeling.

'We are exactly who we should be,' he said, and pulled back. Away from her. 'A king and queen celebrating the union of their nations. The line between what happens when the lamp is lit and what happens here cannot be blurred.'

'The lines have always been blurry for me,' she said. Because they had been. Ever since the church. His stolen kiss. What had happened in her chambers. Nothing had been the same. *She* had not felt the same.

'Not for me,' he said.

'Why would you lie?'

'I am not.'

'You feel it too. Whenever we are together. Whenever—'

He released her. Stepped back. Stood tall. Erect. Present as a king.

Breathless, she stared at him.

'Angelo—'

'*King* Angelo,' he corrected. Two simple words. A title. A name. A definition of who he was and all he would allow her to know.

She would not let her shoulders slump. She would not show him how his dismissal hurt.

She stepped back, away from him, and acknowledged what he wanted her to understand. The only person he would allow her to see. To know.

The King.

'Goodnight, King Angelo,' she said, and dropped to her knees in the deepest curtsey her body would allow.

She arose with her spine straighter and her shoulders wider. Because she understood now, didn't she?

He wanted a queen.

And any queen would do.

She turned, climbed the stairs, walked through the black double doors with their golden hinges, and as they closed behind her she ran.

Fast.

Until she was face to face with her chambers.

She opened the door, closed it behind her and slumped against it. Sank to her bottom, the red ruffles of her dress flaring and puffing around her like a big meringue.

Natalia closed her eyes. Breathed in…breathed out.

Concentrated on the whoosh of her heart in her ears. The proof she was alive. She mattered.

This woman sat on the floor with everything she'd thought she'd wanted—*needed*—and knew that understanding it wasn't enough any more.

She'd thought her single-mindedness was a strength. Her focus would make her strong for her people. For her mother. But she'd been lying to herself all this time. It was a front—a mask to hide the scared little girl beneath.

The girl who was frightened that she wouldn't deserve her father's love unless she proved she was worth it. Worth the loss of her mother…

She'd tucked away those feelings for so long, and now they were all coming to her in a tidal wave. A blanket of old hurts, of missed opportunities for joy, of the life she hadn't lived because she'd refused to see beyond the border. The palace. The debt she needed to repay.

How could she be a strong queen if she didn't feel? If she refused to let herself live the way her mother had? Without fear? Without regret?

The wood of the door shuddered.

A firm, heavy knock reverberated through her whole body.

She wouldn't think. She wouldn't allow herself to hesitate.

She stood. She opened the door and there he was.

'Invite me inside, Natalia.'

Her breathing was heavy. *Harsh.* 'Why?' she asked.

'I want to show you something.'

'I know everything that's inside my rooms,' she said. 'I have seen it all.'

'Not this,' he promised.

Did she believe him? Or was this another game? Another lesson she did not know how to prepare for? How to react to whatever information he would impart in her studies?

Something inside her hurt. Not a sexual pain. Not the ache of unfulfilled desire. But something else.

'The choice is yours,' he said, when words failed her. 'You can turn around and go inside your rooms without me, or you can invite me in and I will show you why you feel what you are feeling. Where this connection between us originated.'

'You know?'

'I do.'

'How?'

'Invite me inside, Natalia,' he said again. 'And I will show you the truth you deserve to see from me,' he said. 'Tell you the story you deserve to know.'

All her life she'd avoided any truth that didn't align with her goals. She hadn't just been asking the wrong questions. She hadn't asked any questions at all. She'd approached her life with one goal, one aim: to restore her mother's dreams to her people. And she'd forgotten everything else. Everyone else. Including herself.

But if she invited him inside it wouldn't be for the Princess she had been or for the Queen he expected her to be.

It would be for her.

Her choice.

'Come in,' she said, and he did, closing the door behind him. 'Now what?'

He dipped his head again. 'There.'

She splayed her hands. 'Where?'

'The mirror.'

Her eyes flitted to the overly large gilded mirror on the back wall.

'Yes, Angelo, it's a looking glass. A common household necessity since long before our times,' she said too sharply. 'It reflects things.'

'And that is exactly what I want you to see.'

'My reflection?'

He walked towards her until feet became a foot and a foot became inches between them.

'*Our* reflection.'

'Why?'

'Go to the mirror, stand in front of it, and I will show you.'

'Show me what?'

'Why there have to be rules between us,' he said.

She moved to the mirror and stood before it. Her cheeks were rosier than before she'd left, but it still showed the same person.

She was still the same on the outside.

But on the inside...

'What am I supposed to see?'

'Nothing yet.'

And then he was behind her. His breath hit her nape.

'Spread your arms.'

She did. She lifted them until, like wings, they splayed at her sides.

'Relax your fingers.'

His fingers slid over her shoulders, along the underside of her arms, and down along her wrists until their palms met. He held the weight of her arms and she felt weightless. *Safe.*

Natalia closed her eyes. She was flying with her feet on the ground.

'Open your eyes,' he commanded. 'What do you see?'

What *did* she see?

A dark king against a blood-red queen.

'I see *us*,' she said.

'Because we are the same.'

'We are the people we usually are.'

'We are the *same*,' he repeated.

'I don't understand,' she said. 'Explain.'

'Three years ago, a king discovered he was supposed to marry a princess,' he said. 'But the King did not want to meet the Princess's father and confirm the terms of his long-arranged marriage. So he sent someone else instead.'

'Who did he send?' she asked quietly, softly, because she didn't want him to stop.

'His twin,' he said. 'His identical twin brother.'

'Couldn't people tell they'd switched places?'

'No one knew when they did it. Not even their father.'

'Two little boys, who had grown into men, and their father couldn't tell them apart?'

'No.'

Her heart broke for those little boys. Her father had always known who she was. Her mother's daughter. The daughter who had stolen everything from him. He had loved her anyway. But hadn't her father also dismissed her individuality? Never let her shine too brightly for fear she would outshine her mother's memory? Or, more fatally, repeat history?

Their eyes locked in the mirror.

'Did they switch often?' she asked.

'All the time.'

'Why?'

'One brother wanted to hide and the other wanted to be seen.'

'Even if it wasn't as himself?'

'Yes.'

The crack in her chest widened. But she waited for his story of two men sharing one life. Knew that even now, as one of those men told her that story, he was still talking about himself in the third person.

'The King's brother went to the castle. He'd negotiated many diplomatic treaties. He'd stood in his brother's stead on so very many official occasions. He hadn't considered this meeting would be any different.'

She waited. Waited for him to tell her how it had been different.

'The palace enchanted him the moment he stepped outside the car. It was a mystical place. Ripped straight out of a fairy tale. And it had secrets.'

'What secrets?' she whispered.

'A hidden princess,' he replied.

'Where was she hiding?'

'He saw the Princess in a garden of lush greens. She was surrounded by a maze of ever-winding tunnels and turns. They'd locked her inside, but she was oblivious. And the recognition of her imprisonment overwhelmed the King's brother.'

'Did he pity her?'

'Oh, no, he didn't pity her.'

'Why not?' she asked. 'If she was trapped?'

'Because she was him.'

Her brow furrowed. 'She was *him*?'

'His mirror image.'

She looked at him standing behind her in their reflection. Standing so close to her they might be one person. One entity.

'She was waiting to be summoned,' he continued. 'Waiting for her father to tell her when was time to do her duty. And that was all the man had ever known, you see. The wait for duty to summon him. He was the spare to the throne. Inconsequential unless he was needed to stand inside someone else's shoes. To look at his brother's soon-to-be wife and want her for himself. He couldn't explain it. The recognition. The knowing that she was meant for him and that it was his duty to free her from the maze and summon her for himself. Not for the King, but for himself.'

Her heart raced. 'But he never did?'

'He couldn't. Because their connection was nothing but an unrequited selfish desire,' he said. 'She didn't know him. Wouldn't have recognised him as anything other than what he was pretending to be. A king come to claim her. Summon her in the name of duty. But her duty was not his to claim. She did not belong to him.'

Her eyes clouded over. Misted. And she didn't know who she wanted to cry for. For the Princess in the garden, who had never known she'd been seen, or the man who had seen her and never tried to tell her. *Show her*.

This was the recognition she'd felt the moment she'd seen him inside the church on their wedding day. When she'd stolen a kiss. When she'd begged him to kiss her again…

'She would have known it was you,' she said.

'If he'd gone to her…revealed himself…he would have not only betrayed his duty, and his brother. He would have betrayed her, too.'

'How?'

'He would have seduced her.'

A blush crept up her chest as bright and as vivid as her dress.

'It wouldn't have been a betrayal if she'd wanted to be seduced.'

'Oh, it would have.'

He leaned in closer, until the press of him triggered a wave of arousal. And she tingled. All over. Between her legs.

'He would have made her forget her role. Her duty. Just as he forgot his with one look—one glance—in her direction. He wanted her, and he almost betrayed everything he believed in because of her.'

She couldn't turn back time, but she could turn around now. Face him. *See* him.

She turned, and he let her arms fall.

A tear splashed onto the front of her dress. Darkening the red.

Two firm but gentle fingers lifted her chin. 'Why are you crying?'

She looked up into his face. Into the razor-sharp lines of the face of a man who had shared a story. *His* story. *Their* story. Told her where it had all begun.

And she had never known. Would never have guessed.

'Do not pity the man, Princess,' he said. 'He has all he could ever have wished for. By default, he has won. The crown. The Princess. And now she feels it too. A physical reaction for reasons unexplained. Unknown. It's just *there*. It has always been there.'

'How do you know she feels it too?' she asked.

Because she wanted him to say it. To turn this story told in the third person into the present tense. Into the now.

'Because she is *you*.'

CHAPTER EIGHT

ANGELO HELD HIS breath and waited for it. For her denial. For her rejection. For her logical response.

He knew his story was illogical.

Fantastical.

He waited for her to clarify what he already knew. That his story was nothing but the overactive imagination of a man who should never have looked down into those gardens. Should never have let his gaze linger.

Because she was never meant to be his.

They'd never been the same—never could be—because he'd misunderstood her status. Who and what she was. Because she had been born to be a queen. The Queen who had stood before her people and sworn to bring them untold strength. The Queen who had charmed as easily as she breathed air at the coronation meal and the coronation ball.

But her rejection wasn't coming.

Because he'd won, hadn't he?

By default.

Not in the gardens, and not after that, but here—in this moment. Because between his thumb and his forefinger he'd captured a true fairy tale princess.

His misrepresented fantasy had captivated her—seduced her.

A lie. A twisted tale of the truth because he hadn't been able to let her go.

Downstairs, he'd thought she'd found him out. Realised he was an imposter in their marriage. That she'd made promises to a man who was seducing her for his own ends. A trick. A tease.

Because he'd let her believe he had always been this man. Her match.

A king.

And he'd known the minute his foot had hit the first of those thirteen stairs as he went to find her that he'd seduce her.

Tonight.

Before she did as he'd told her and found out the truth on her own. Asked the right questions. Opened her personal laptop and typed in his name. Saw things. Ugly things. Discovered how his greed for self-gratification had killed the *real* King.

His twin.

An acrid heat rose in his throat. His chest burnt. His stomach twisted.

He should have let her go.

He should not have chased her. Chased the compulsion in his gut to give her another narrative. Another truth to believe. *To know.*

That *this* was her destiny.

He was her match.

Always had been.

But he couldn't help himself. Because this was who he was. He hadn't been born to be anything but a substitute. A stand-in. A spare. A selfish manipulator. A crown-stealer. A man who won by default.

And tonight he would win again.

Whatever it took.

Whatever she wanted to know, he would tell her.

He would turn his grotesque past into something palatable. Whatever pretty words she needed to hear— he would say them. And when all the words had been said…when she was content…she would welcome him into her bed and he would drive himself inside her until the burn in his body evaporated as if it had never existed.

When she found out the truth it wouldn't matter. Because whatever this was between them would be over.

His fingers tightened on her chin. 'Invite me inside.'

Her eyes widened, but they still glistened. Just for him. For the lie she believed was true.

He was hers. And she was his.

Destiny.

'You are inside,' she said.

But he wasn't inside deeply enough, was he?

He loosened his grip, allowed his fingers to graze along her jawline, down her delicate neck. He let his hand rest there. Around her throat. He didn't tighten his fingers. Didn't squeeze. Didn't show her how for three years her grip around his throat had placed him in a choke-hold.

He didn't tell her how for three long years he hadn't been able to breathe. Hadn't been able to fill his lungs with the air he needed. Because the air he had needed to inhale was *her*.

And right now he was breathing.

However twisted his fairy tale, his retelling of what

had actually happened had released something inside him. A tension. The death grip of desire was lifting from his shoulders. The fingers around his throat were easing...

He closed his eyes. Dipped his head. Placed his mouth to her ear and breathed. Deeply. Until for the first time he felt full. Complete.

It was agony. Yet delicious. His acceptance that *this* was what he needed.

Her.

Because he was selfish. And tonight he would embrace his greed. Eat until he was full. Until he knew the ache in his gut would never reappear because he'd feasted too greedily. Too wantonly.

'Invite me into your bedroom.'

She gasped.

He dragged in a deeper breath. Let her flower scent take root in his gut. Because tonight he would let it bloom.

'Take me to bed, Princess,' he hissed rawly. 'Because you want me there. Because you choose *me* as I chose you that day in the garden. Invite me inside your body because you have no other choice. Because you feel it too. This pull. This ache. This agony.'

His breath was hot inside his mouth. And the words were even hotter as they left his lips and entered her ear.

They burnt.

And he watched the fire spread.

Watched her throat tighten. Heard the flames hiss in her accelerated breath.

And, oh, it would be so easy to end this now. Surrender himself to the fire and place his mouth on her skin. To suck. To bite. To make her want until she didn't need to surrender with words. But he wanted words tonight. Needed them.

In this fantasy there was a choice.

All he needed to do was talk, ask for what he wanted, and it could be his.

All of it.

He wanted to pretend for one night that it had always been meant to be his.

He lifted his head and let his hand fall away from her throat. He met her heated gaze with his own and let himself drown in her eyes. In the lie he found there. The lie he was seducing her with. And he would speak it. Say the words that would be his ultimate seduction. The ultimate betrayal of his innocent forbidden princess.

'This is destiny,' he said huskily, feeding the lie, letting it grow between them until he almost believed it himself. 'We were always meant to stand here. In front of one another. Wanting each other. Choosing this instinct. *Chemistry.* You were always meant to choose me. So choose me now. Choose *this*.'

Such a convincing liar was he. Because his words felt true. In his mouth. On his lips.

It was a desperate plea for her to choose him. And it was true, wasn't it? This disgusting need inside him to be seen—wanted for himself—regardless of the consequences. Because he was too needy. Too greedy.

Too selfish *not* to do this. Not to claim her as himself. Not as the King, not as anything other than the man he had been in those gardens. A man reaching above his station. Beyond his status. To touch what was untouchable.

Just once.

'No,' she said.

His stomach dropped to the floor.

'No?' he repeated.

Her eyes searched his. Her pink-flushed cheeks were pinched in consternation. Her flawless brow furrowed with deep lines.

'Not like this.'

She backed up—moved away from him—taking his breath with her. Stealing it when he needed it to survive this moment—this night. And it took everything in him—*everything*—not to reach out. To drag her body against his and kiss her. Seduce her with his mouth on hers and make her choose this.

Choose *him*.

But how could she?

However detailed the lie. However tantalising the tale. He was nothing more than a substitute. A stand-in. An imposter who needed a queen.

And she could see it now, couldn't she? Just as he could see her. Recognise who she was.

She was a queen. It lived in her DNA. In the very essence of her. She was not the woman he'd convinced himself he'd seen in the gardens, but the woman standing in front of him.

Natalia.

Not the idealised version he'd painted in his mind—because she was not *that* woman. She was so much more than he'd imagined. She was not his counterpart. They were not the same. She cared. For it all. For her people. For her duty.

For *him*.

For the lie of him. The misrepresentation of a man he could never be. Because he'd exposed too much.

Made the lie too complicated. And now she could see straight through it.

Her breathing was as harsh and fast as his own. They stared at each other across the space she'd put between them.

'Take off your crown.'

Her words were a husky demand. The demand of a queen directing her subordinate.

He braced himself for the blow.

For her rejection of him. Of the lie. Because she could see the truth now. See the man he had always been.

This wasn't her destiny.

He wasn't her destiny.

He was a usurper. He'd stolen his brother's life the way he'd always wanted to steal her. And now she would expose him.

He didn't reply. He couldn't speak.

He reached up and took off the cold crown. The symbol of the life that should never have been his—of the man he never should have become.

He held it out to her.

His fingers trembled, and he locked his jaw. Gritted his teeth. Waited for her to take it. To admonish him. *Out him.*

'Put it there.'

She dipped her head to the side table beside him and he put it down. The crown. The lie. The fantasy.

And then, like the boy he'd been in his father's office, pretending to be Luciano, he went back to his spot to take his punishment. But this time the punishment was his. Because the crime was his and his alone.

He held steady. Held her gaze.

Her hands rose at her sides until her fingers grazed the lower tier of diamonds on her crown. Her fingers pressed into them. Into the precious symbolic metal on her head.

She lifted it until it floated above her head. Her red-covered chest was rising and falling with the speed of his own. She took it off.

And he couldn't read her. Didn't know how to understand the look in her eyes that made him want to get on his knees and beg her to end this agony.

To expose him quickly.

To end his misery.

She meant to strip him of his crown. Expose every lie he had ever built around himself. And he deserved it. For risking the lie to claim her.

It was what he deserved. To be degraded. To be humiliated. To be punished for his crimes.

She lifted her shoulders and his eyes zoned in on her lips. He watched them part. Readied himself for the ultimate rejection. For her to speak the truth.

He was a liar.

A fraud.

Her lips parted and he waited for the whip.

'If we had met in those gardens… If you had come to me…' Her words were quick, her breathing faster. 'This is what I would have seen. I would have *felt* it.'

And he couldn't help it. He broke the spell and spoke.

'What are you doing, Princess?'

'Choosing,' she said huskily, and she placed her crown next to his and moved back.

'Choosing what?' he asked. Because he had not expected this. Whatever *this* was.

Something in her gaze shifted, moved, deepened.

'If you had made a different choice... If you had re-vealed yourself to me three years ago... *This* is what we would have been.'

'What?' he growled, his agony intense. '*What* would we have been?'

'Equal.'

What trick was this?

'Equal?' he repeated.

'I was not a queen. I wasn't anything in those gar-dens but a woman waiting for her life to begin,' she explained. She placed her hands to the centre of her chest. 'I never thought there were any other choices for me. My choices were bullet-pointed. Chosen be-cause of the circumstances of my birth. But I realise now there were other choices. I just didn't see them. But I would have seen *you*. Felt *this*. Our connection. I would have felt *you*.'

His instinct was to tell her the truth. It was sex. Lust. *Desire.* But he couldn't. If he did, he would have to tell her everything. Break this spell he was casting over her and reveal the truth of the man standing in front of her.

That it was all his fault. The kingdom's downfall. His brother's death. Because he had chosen his own needs above everything else. His need to be out in a world that would see him and know his name.

Tonight, she would know his name. Scream it. Taste every syllable. He'd take his pleasure. Give her endless pleasure in return. And he would put it into his mem-ory. The sound of her. The feel. Because he would allow himself tonight. Only tonight. And then he would snatch it all away from her by revealing his seduction. Tell-ing her that was it. One night was all they could have.

He'd awaken her to the only choice available to him.

The crown or her. And he would choose the crown. His duty. He couldn't have both because she was right. The lines between duty and desire were blurred. They had *always* been blurred with her.

He wouldn't make the wrong choice again.

He would choose correctly.

It would hurt her, but it would be quick. She would heal. He would make sure of it. Because she was right. She had a right to know. To know this was who he was.

A glutton.

Who desired only the forbidden.

He wanted her so desperately because she was never meant to be his.

Even after everything.

His brother's death.

Damn himself to hell, he *wanted* her.

So he remained silent. Still. And let her pull him deeper into the fantasy. Into the lie that said this was anything other than what it really was.

A seduction.

Despite the blush spreading from her heaving chest up her throat, to heat her cheeks, she raised her chin. Met his gaze.

'And I choose *this*,' she breathed. 'I choose *this* destiny. I choose the two people standing here, in front of each other. The people we would have been in the garden. And I would like you…'

She swallowed. Repeatedly. And he would not reach out. He would not pull her to him.

'What would you like, Natalia?' he asked. Because he wanted words. Her words. He wanted her to explain what she was choosing.

'I want you to take me to bed,' she said.

By God, he was hard. At the sight of her. At the unexpectedness of whatever was happening between them. Whatever *she* was making happen between them.

He wasn't the seducer any more.

She was.

And he understood what he must do. Understood what she was doing. And something inside his chest ached. Not a sexual ache. But the sweet and bitter pain of a healing wound.

He shrugged off his jacket and it thumped to the floor. He removed his tie. Unbuttoned his shirt. Kicked off his shoes. Tore free the buckle on his belt, pushed down his trousers. His boxers. Unclipped his sock braces and pulled his feet free from his silk socks.

He stepped out of the puddle of clothes at his feet and stood before her in his skin. Naked. Exposed.

She didn't move towards him. Didn't speak. But she looked at him. Moved her gaze over his shoulders, his chest, the intimate section of his body between his legs, brushing against his stomach.

And he heard her gasp. Caught the tremble moving over her skin. Could hear the awe in each delicate rasp being drawn between her parted lips.

'Natalia…' He couldn't finish—couldn't ask her to complete this fantasy she was gifting him. To fulfil his need to be equal with her in all ways.

But she knew, didn't she? Because she reached for the fabric at her collarbone with trembling fingers and tugged until it was dislodged. Exposed her creamy shoulders. She kept tugging until her arms were free. Then she peeled the dress down, revealed her small, perfect breasts and kept tugging it down, until her skirts puffed around her hips.

She placed her fingers inside her skirts and pushed them down. The ruffles. The lace. Until the dress glistening with diamonds pooled around her feet.

And she stood before him, naked but for her red panties.

He was seduced. *Completely.* Locked into this fantasy he was sharing with Natalia. A woman standing as proud and graceful as the Queen she was even now, without her clothes...

'Come to me,' he demanded.

And she did.

She stepped out of the red puffs at her feet and came to him. Still wearing her red silken heels.

He dropped to his knees. Careful not to let his fingers touch her skin, Angelo unbuckled the silver straps that locked her shoes to her ankles.

'Lean on my shoulder and step out of your shoes, Princess,' he said huskily at her feet. Keeping his eyes down. On her shoes.

He waited for her touch on him.

She touched him. Applied pressure to his shoulder.

And his body screamed at him to take her hand, pull her down to the floor with him and end this now. Thrust himself inside her willing body and lose his head. Forget it all and be with her. The way he had always longed to be...

But he couldn't.

His fantasy—the fantasy she was gifting him—was not complete. So he pulled off her shoes. Placed each bare foot on the ground before him and stood.

His bold virgin trembled before him.

'Angelo—'

'Shush...' He shook his head. 'Your panties.'

He swallowed down his urge to hurry—because this needed to be slow. She needed to finish what she'd started. Because he understood now. What she was doing for him.

'Take them off.'

And slowly she did. She hooked her fingers into the waistband of her panties and pushed them to the floor.

Breathless, his chest heaving, he said, 'Now we are equal, aren't we?'

She nodded. A graceful confirmation. Although her cheeks burnt.

And he needed no other words. No other form of consent.

Tonight she was his.

Tonight they were equal.

Free to choose.

And he chose the lie—*the fantasy*—and he cupped her cheeks, looked into the green lagoons of her eyes, with their endless depths, and let himself drown.

Natalia felt it. The understanding that this was right. This was the way it should always have been. Because she could *see* him. And for the first time in her life she could see herself.

All her life she'd thought her destiny was a crown, but it wasn't.

It was him.

The man who had made her expose the woman she'd never thought existed. Never considered. But here she was. Alive and breathing in the arms of a man she'd never considered either.

Naked. With no symbols of what they were out-

side these rooms. No flames or frustration. No rules
to guide them.

Just this.

An unexplainable connection.

She wasn't nervous. She didn't feel vulnerable without her material defences. She felt reborn in the safety
of the hands cupping her cheeks so softly, so carefully.

So tenderly.

And his mouth was just there.

Waiting.

Not for a stolen kiss or a requested one. But a kiss
neither of them could deny.

So she didn't speak. She didn't announce what would
happen next and neither did he.

Because it was destiny.

Preordained.

They moved as instinct dictated. Towards one another.
Until their lips stilled a heartbeat from each other's. And
they breathed. Inhaled each other. Until the last milli-
metre disappeared.

Their lips met.

His tongue pierced between her lips and she pressed
her chest against his. Pushed her heavy breasts and her
aching nipples into the warm heat of his body, drove her
fingers into his hair. Pulled him closer. *Nearer.*

'Natalia…'

'Angelo!' she moaned each syllable. Deeply. Loudly.
Freely.

A sound rumbled in his chest. And then his hands
were leaving her face, moving down her back to cup
her bottom. He lifted her.

'Wrap your legs around me,' he demanded breathlessly into her mouth, and she did. She wrapped her legs around his waist.

His mouth hovering above hers, he moved. His stomach shifted against the heart of her. Her fingers flexed. Her nails dug into the muscles of his broad shoulders.

It was too much and not enough.

'Angelo!'

She locked her ankles in the small of his back. Drew his body closer, harder against the sensitive section between her thighs, and delighted in her body.

She clung to him, her intimate muscles tightening, wanting more than the friction of his skin. Wanting release.

He opened her bedroom door and twisted their bodies until she was sitting on his lap as he sat on the edge of the mattress. Her open legs hugged his hips as he sat between them and she could feel the heat of his arousal beneath her. Hard and silken.

She could see nothing. Feel nothing. Nothing but him.

His eyes wild, he said, 'Rock against me.'

'Against you?'

'Use my body to find your pleasure. The way you did with my hand,' he reminded her. 'My mouth.'

The ache in her belly swelled.

His cheeks were stained a deep red. He gripped her hips. 'Like this,' he said, and moved his thickness against her.

She closed her eyes. 'Oh…'

He moved her. Dragged her hips slowly backwards and forwards. Until her back arched, her head thrown back in this unexpected ecstasy.

And then he was kissing her chest. The valley between her breasts. Soft and yet hard kisses rained all over her, and then his mouth clamped onto her nipple. He sucked her into his mouth.

'*Oh!*' she cried out. Needing more. Wanting more. Needing everything he could give her. 'Faster, please,' she begged. 'Faster.'

He didn't deny her. His fingers pressed into her hipbones and he rocked her. Faster. Harder. Against his swollen length. Until she was moving on her own. Following the urge of her body, she pressed down. Moved herself. Rocked against him until her she didn't know where he began and she ended.

He tore his mouth from her breast. 'Look at me.'

Breathless, unable to stop the movement of her hips, she looked down. At him.

'Faster, Princess,' he said huskily.

She moved faster, with wild abandon, giving in to the pleasures of her body. To the pleasures he was gifting her. To the control of them. The choice to find what she wanted. To name it, claim it and possess it.

And she wanted this.

Him.

Only him.

She couldn't help it. She closed her eyes.

'Angelo, I'm—'

'Come, Princess,' he encouraged breathlessly. 'For *me.*'

She exploded. Fireworks bursting behind her eyelids in Technicolor. It was beautiful. It was life. It was living. It was choosing to experience all she had been denying herself.

Pleasure.

Love.

She opened her eyes.

Love?

Natalia looked at him. *Really* looked. At the man, at the King, who was already her teacher, her mentor, a complicated friend.

Her husband.

She feathered her fingers across his jaw, across his cheeks. Gazed into eyes so dark they shone. Did they shine for her? For desire? Or for something more?

Her heart thudded. Was this love? Not just sex? But connection? Two magnets snapping together because it was what was supposed to happen?

Science. Destiny. A combination of the two. Who knew? She didn't. But…

Natalia clamped her hands to his face and thrust her tongue into his mouth. He deepened the kiss. Cradling her skull as she cradled his face.

'I need you,' he growled, and shifted their positions until she lay on her back and he was above her. Between her thighs.

'I need you too,' she said. Rawly. Honestly. *'Now.'*

His face was a maze of conflict. Tension radiating from every etched line of concentration.

She placed her hand on his cheek. 'Ease the pain for us both,' she pleaded, giving him permission to forget himself. To forget everything but the here and now as she wanted to do.

She needed to focus on nothing but her body. His body. Theirs was a connection that ran deeper than physical pleasures, she realised. Because it was bone-deep.

'Natalia…'

'Now, Angelo.' She raised her hips, as her body demanded, and pressed herself against the tip of his hardness. *'Please.'*

A roar exploded from his lips and he thrust himself inside her. She roared too. Roared with the expansion of her most intimate self. Revelling in the fullness. The completeness.

And then he moved. Pushing deeper inside her. And she was weightless. Ready to break free from her earthly bonds and fly.

'You are beautiful,' he said, looking down into her eyes, and she saw herself reflected in his sincere honesty.

She felt beautiful.

'And so are you,' she replied—because he was. He *was* beautiful. He'd gifted her a story. Trusted her with *his* story. A fairy tale of their beginnings.

He'd seduced her.

Made love to her.

And there was that word again.

Love.

If it was love, it didn't hurt. There was no pain. Only warmth. Only certainty that his body belonged inside hers.

Was *that* love?

'Faster, my king,' she encouraged him, just as he'd encouraged her. 'Faster, my husband.' Her hands gripped his face. Made him look at her as she was looking at him. 'My Angelo.'

Oh, no.

Those words felt good. Right. *Electrifying.*

His brow was covered in a sheen of sweat.

His face was at war. All tight lines of conflicted pleasure and pain.

And she was just as conflicted. Because her body screamed that she was his. Only his. But her mind... her heart...

Were they his too?

'Faster,' she panted. *'Please.'*

And he did move faster. He gripped her hips and drove inside her until no thoughts were left in her head. Only sensation. Only pleasure. And she could barely draw breath with the beautiful agony of it all. Of him inside her. His beautiful body making her feel.

'You are perfect,' he said huskily. 'You are everything and more than I ever imagined.'

He claimed her lips. His body pumped, hard and fast, until her name flew from his mouth.

'Natalia!'

A delicious heat spilled inside her. Her abdomen tightened. Her intimate muscles squeezed. Taking him deeper.

'Angelo!'

She was lost. Lost to pleasure. And there they met. In the garden. Surrendering to instinct. To destiny.

Natalia pulled him closer and he came to her until their bodies pressed together. Chest to chest. Heaving. Breathing in sync.

She closed her eyes and let him in. Welcomed him to the place where they should have met. A place of honesty. Of raw vulnerability. Because then they would have been able to choose. As they were choosing now.

To hold each other.

Just as they were.

Equal.

'Thank you,' she whispered into his ear. And she

meant it. 'It was everything and more I could have ever wished for. But… I want more.'

And she did. Because those feelings were still there. A lightness. A heaviness. A knowing.

She'd felt them on their wedding day. In the study. At her coronation. *Tonight.*

Was this what it had been like for her parents? This instinctual need to be with the other person regardless of duty? Regardless of anything?

Her fingers dug into his shoulders despite herself and she clung to him. To Angelo. To the man between her thighs, breaking her apart and putting her back together in a way she wasn't ready for.

Had her parents chosen each other and supported each other regardless of their faults because they hadn't been able to deny it? Science? Chemical reaction? Destiny?

Love?

Was she falling in love with him?

Had she fallen so far, so fast, so deeply, she hadn't realised what was happening?

Her heart raged inside her chest. Beating harder. *Faster.* Was it urging her to set it free and give it to him?

What if she gave it to him?

What if this *was* love?

'More?' he asked huskily.

'Yes,' she said. Because she did want more. So much more—didn't she?

She wanted *all* of him.

Arousal stirred again, instantly and strongly, in her stomach.

So she said the only words she could.

'I want to do it again.'

CHAPTER NINE

AND SO DID HE.

He was still inside her. On top of her. Pressed against every silken part of her body as he'd imagined.

His seduction was complete, and yet his body stirred. Again. Wanting. Needing to show her every delight he could teach her.

And he knew what kept his head buried in the crook of her neck. Inhaling her. What kept his weight resting on his elbows but staying close, *so close*. Her heart thudded against his. Their chests rose and fell, met and descended, to meet again.

He knew why he couldn't pull himself from her body and look at her.

Fear.

It tingled in his senses. The knowing that once was not enough. Would *never* be enough.

If he spoke, if he raised his head and saw the same desire reflected in her gaze, he would take her again. And again. Until they were both broken from their desire. Too physically exhausted to draw breath.

His desire would kill them both.

He shifted. Only slightly. Because his body wouldn't—*couldn't*—remain still. And she moaned. A deep whine into his ear. Her intimate muscles squeezed around his thickening length. Her body knew, didn't it? Even without his words.

He was lost. Damned for ever to be selfish. *Greedy.* His gut twisted and he closed his eyes tightly. Shut out the drag on his senses. The need. The ache. To do it all again. Love her body. Worship it as it deserved.

But it was her first time, and she would be sore.

His focus zapped, razor-sharp. He lifted himself and began to withdraw.

'No,' he said, and groaned. It was agony. Pulling himself from the one place his body wanted to be. Inside her. 'No more.'

'Wait.' Her hands moved to his shoulders. Halting him. 'Please.'

He did. He waited. Inside her. Raised above her. He turned his head and met her eyes with his. And there it was.

Desire.

In her glazed green eyes. In her pink flushed cheeks. Exhaled from her parted lips.

How easy it would be to lower his head. To claim her mouth and her body all over again. And she would meet him, he knew. In their desire, thrust for thrust. Because she matched him.

In bed.

But what of outside it?

When this night was over and she tip-tapped into her little computer and asked questions he wouldn't give her answers to?

She would read of his abandonment not only of his brother, but of his people. Of his duties. Of the charities he'd ignored when they'd asked for his presence.

His endorsement. And what of the people those charities benefited? He had abandoned them all. He hadn't cared for any of them. Hadn't wanted to let himself care. Because he was a blight on all of them. The lives his endorsement would have saved. The life of his brother that he could have saved if only he'd stayed where his duty dictated.

No, this had to be the end—whether or not his body knew it.

He would make it so.

'You need a bath, Princess,' he declared, and he moved over her, off her, and she let him go.

With his back to her, he closed his eyes, inhaled deeply. Shifting his focus. Remembering who he had to be before he drowned in the fantasy.

He would never be equal to her in this life. Because he'd stolen this life. His brother's life. His brother's wife. His queen. The scales were not balanced. They never had been. Never would be. Even if he wished it could be different. Even if this night has shown him the pleasure that a different life could bring.

The mattress shifted. He did not open his eyes. Would not watch her walk to the bathroom. But his ears pricked and he allowed himself to listen. He waited for the pad of her bare feet. For her to leave him.

But she didn't. She laid her hand gently on his back.

'I don't want a bath,' she said.

He gritted his teeth and made himself open his eyes, tilt his head until she came into his peripheral vision.

'You need one,' he said. 'Your body will be sore.'

'My body is fine,' she said.

'A bath is required,' he hissed, too harshly.

Because he needed her to leave...because he was not sure he could.

'*I* will choose when I have a bath, for how long, and with how many bubbles,' she corrected, and it came to him like a thump to the brain.

That day in the study, when he'd told her to decide for herself when she wanted to bathe because she was Queen.

And here she was. A queen without clothes. Without her crown.

The Queen she had been destined to become and the Queen she had grown into in a few short weeks.

'Angelo,' she said.

And his name was a declaration of what he would always be, regardless of what he'd stolen. Just a man. A greedy man.

'Look at me,' she demanded. But he heard the tremble. The shudder of hesitation. 'Please, look at me.'

He made himself move his body. Turn it until he knelt before her. And there she was. Her hair mussed. Her cheeks still flushed. Her pink-tipped breasts exposed and proud.

'I'm not having a bath,' she told him. 'I don't want one. I need...*you*.'

'No,' he growled. Too deeply.

Because his brain was screaming, *She chose you!* and it was a lie. She could not choose him because she did not know him.

'You don't need me,' he finished, because it was a truth she would realise when he left her tonight. No lie. No fantastical fantasy. Only the raw and naked truth.

'But I...' she croaked, and it nearly undid him.

Her shoulders rose just as her hands did.

'I still feel things,' she said, and placed her hands between her breasts. 'In here. And they're too intense. Too obscure…' Her hands dropped into her lap. 'I don't understand what is happening. I don't—' She swallowed. Hard. 'I—'

'It's not sex you need,' he told her, because it was true. He knew it. Although it would be the easiest thing in the world to distract her with it. To bury himself in her and make them both forget. Because if he made love to her again, he'd never stop.

'Tell me,' she said, biting on her swollen bottom lip. 'What is it I need to make these feelings…*stop*?'

'Not sex.'

'Then what?'

He tensed.

'Will you hold me?' she asked.

'Hold you?'

'In your arms.'

'Why?'

'Because I am emotional,' she admitted, and her lips moved.

It was a gentle tug of her mouth and he saw the quiver. The vulnerability.

'Because I'm tired of trying to understand this connection between us. Because I need you to hold me.'

She didn't wait. She moved towards him and he braced himself.

Braced for contact.

And then she was on him.

Wrapping her arms around him.

His arms splayed in the air at his sides and he held his breath.

'Hold me,' she urged.

And he couldn't help it. He did.

He leaned in and pulled her to him. Into his chest. And he did what he would have done if he'd been a better man.

He held her. They held each other.

Her arms were wrapped around him, her head on his chest.

And he loathed it. Loathed how this felt more intimate than being inside her.

Never had he embraced a lover—not with anything but the need to drive out the demons inside him. He'd never given or sought comfort. Never wanted it. But she was so soft against him. So pliant. He couldn't help it. He pulled her closer. Held her tighter.

And it felt...*right*.

'I'm sorry,' she said into his chest.

He tensed. 'There's nothing to be sorry for,' he said against her head, and he buried his nose into her hair.

Because there wasn't. This was all on him. He'd taken what he wanted and hadn't thought about the immediate aftermath. The personal emotional toll his greed would take on another person.

He never did.

Never had.

Not when it mattered.

Until now.

His hands moved over the centre of her back. Stroking. Soothing. He placed his fingers on her elbows and pulled gently.

'Wrap your arms around my neck,' he instructed, and she shifted until her eyes caught his.

She nodded and wrapped her arms around his neck. And that thing in his chest, caged by bone, thumped.

Hard. Because there it was. Something he hadn't asked for. Didn't want.

Trust.

He scooped her up and got off the bed. She clung to him. He pulled back the covers and deposited her in the centre of the bed, her head against the plump pillows he hadn't bothered to use when he'd claimed her. He'd just put her beneath him and—

'Are you leaving?'

He couldn't—not now.

'No,' he said rawly, and got in beside her. 'Turn on your side.'

'Why?'

'I will show you.'

She shifted, and he pulled her bottom into his hips. Moved his head until hers was beneath his chin. And he spooned her.

'Can we talk?' she asked.

He covered them both with the blanket. 'Talk?'

'Yes,' she confirmed.

He felt the tension leave her body as she pressed into him. She exhaled heavily. A sound that he couldn't define as anything but contentedness.

'Tell me another story.'

'I've told you the only story I had to tell,' he said, because the rest of it wasn't anything he could twist into something palatable.

'Tell me about the lamp,' she said, and grabbed his hand, dragged his arm over her body on top of the blanket. Stroked his forearm. Slowly. Tenderly.

'It is an antique,' he said.

'But why did you need to light it?'

'Because it was dark.'

'That's not what I mean, and you know it.'

He did. 'It was our nightly routine…' he said.

What was he doing? Was he really about to tell her his origin story?

'When did it begin?' she pushed.

And it felt so intimate. Whispering with her in the dark.

'It started when we were seven. Maybe younger.' He swallowed. 'Luciano had got some of his training wrong—not recited some Latin poem from memory—and he'd blamed me for not reciting it for him.'

'Blamed you?' she asked. 'Why?'

'Because it was my fault. Our father could not tell us apart. We were identical. We'd swapped places that day,' he explained. 'And that day I was not in the mood for Latin.'

'He really didn't recognise you?'

'I was not important,' he dismissed easily. Too easily. Because it was the truth.

'You were his son…'

'I was not the heir.'

'What happened?' she asked quietly.

'That night Luciano and I did not talk,' he said. 'We fought with open fists. Neither of us cared who was the heir or the spare. We were boys. *Brothers.* Angry brothers. There were no winners that night. But we realised that the physical release gave us both victory. That night we found a way out.'

'What does that have to do with the lamp?' she asked, confused. 'Or the rules?'

'We refined it. Found release without the bruises. Because a future king cannot have bruises on his face. We lit the lamp, let it burn, and for as long as it did we were not spares or heirs. We were brothers. Duty remained firmly on the other side of the door.'

'And then he died?'

'He did.'

'And you didn't want to light it again?' she asked. 'You didn't want to close the door on duty without him? Not after his death?'

'Yes.'

Her small hand covered his. 'I'm so sorry for your loss, Angelo,' she said, and applied pressure. Squeezed his hand. 'I understand now,' she said.

'Understand what?' he asked, and regretted it instantly. He'd given her permission to delve deeper. To unmask him in the dark for the man he was.

'In the day, our bruises must not show,' she summarised. 'Whatever gives us release in the dark, it must stay there.'

'Exactly.' The rawness in his voice was palpable. 'And it is my duty to protect both of you. The woman you're discovering and the Queen you were born to be.'

'And who protects you?'

'Natalia…' he said huskily.

Was it a warning? A plea? Angelo didn't know.

'I thought my duty was all that could matter. My crown. My people. But this whole week I've spent alone I've got to know parts of myself—to *feel* things I didn't know I could feel—because of you. All week I've thought I could separate my wants from my duty as easily as I can take off my crown,' she said. 'But tonight…'

'Tonight?'

'I couldn't,' she admitted. 'I have wants. Needs. They don't vanish because I tell them to. They didn't disappear because you made a rule that said I could only feel them when we lit a lamp and gave ourselves permission to feel them.'

'You do not know what I feel,' he rasped.

She couldn't. Because despite this intimacy…his *honesty*…he still hadn't revealed himself. His full undisclosed callousness.

'But I do, don't I? Because we are the same. Duty summoned us. Thrust us together. But I'm not a different person because now I'm a queen, am I? I'm still that woman in the garden, and you are still that man. We are not different people when we put on a crown or light a lamp.'

'No,' he rasped. 'We are different because we have to be.'

'You're wrong. I don't think we have to be anything. Because really we aren't. It's a show. *A lie.* Because here in the dark, or in a room full of people, you are the King who held my hand and the man who taught me how to feel for myself. For no one else but *myself.* Why should we pretend to be anyone other than who we are?' she asked. 'Why do we need permission to be ourselves? We are those people, with feelings and needs, regardless of our positions. Our titles. *Our duty.*'

He closed his eyes.

Tomorrow, he would tell her everything. Because she deserved the truth. He would make her see that this was not who he was and why he could never be. Why they could never be a team behind closed doors.

But tonight…

He pushed his nose into her hair. Dragged her body into his. And blocked it all out. Her words. Her thinking that she understood what she couldn't.

'No more talking. Close your eyes, Princess,' he said.

And he knew what he was doing. What he was asking for.

For the fantasy to continue.

For just a little longer.

'Sleep,' he commanded, and he listened to her breathing until it became deep and rhythmic.

And he forgave himself for extending the lie. The fantasy. For closing his eyes…for letting himself fall asleep and pretend that this was how he was always meant to be.

Lost in her arms.

CHAPTER TEN

IT WAS LOVE.

Natalia knew.

She lay still and tried to keep her breathing deep enough to feign sleep and not alert him that she was awake. Because she wanted to look. To stare uninhibitedly at the man who had not only awoken her body, but her mind. Her heart.

She recognised the butterflies fluttering beneath her skin for what they were now.

What they had always been.

And they danced for him.

A swarm beneath her skin.

A warmth in her bloodstream.

Love.

How could it not be? It was a truth, she recognised, as honest as their stolen kiss a few weeks ago. A truth he had felt before she'd even known of his existence.

She itched to pull her palm from where it was placed on his chest, cocooned between their bodies, beneath the blanket, and stroke his cheek. To soothe the tension that even in sleep contorted his face into harsh, beautiful lines of concentration.

How hard he must have concentrated to hide not only himself, but his feelings.

And yet last night he'd listened as she'd babbled her confusion. Held her to him, and told her the story of the lamp, of his brother. She'd asked him questions only he could answer, and when he had not known the answers he'd held her *tighter*. All night. Soothed her. Her racing mind, her aching body.

She moved. Reached up and placed her palm to his face and soothed the itch. *Almost*. She leaned in until her lips were above his and let her eyes drift closed. Let herself relive the agony of waiting. Of how different the waiting had felt with him holding her hand. Guiding her. Teaching her.

With closed lips, she pushed her mouth against his. He stirred against her. She pulled away. And any air left in her lungs halted, neither an exhalation nor an inhalation. It just stayed where it was. Because there, in his deep brown eyes, she could see it.

Not desire.

Love.

'Will you come with me?' she asked. 'Will you come to Vadelto with me?'

His eyes flashed. 'Why?'

'I want to show you something.'

'I have seen all I need to see of your country for now, Princess.'

'Not this,' she promised, as he had last night when he'd asked her to stand in front of the mirror.

'We will take a shower—'

'No,' she said, because she did not want him to leave her. To wash off their mingled scents. The scents of the man and woman they were, regardless of what finery they wore. What sparkly jewels.

'I will make arrangements for later this month.'

'We leave now,' she said. Because if they left this bedroom apart, if she let the night turn into day, she would lose this man. She knew. This moment would be lost. Hidden beneath the rules.

He frowned. 'We will need to alert the staff, the Vadelton palace, your father—'

'We aren't going to the palace,' she corrected. 'All we need is a car, and I will alert the people who need to know of our arrival.'

'I'll go to my chambers and change—'

'We will wear our clothes from the ball.'

His jaw set. 'Princess—'

'Please,' she pleaded. Because this was it. This was the only way to show him that they had never been hidden from anyone but themselves.

'Okay, Natalia.'

The Adam's apple in his throat moved heavily. Up and down. The tension in his jaw beneath her fingers still cupping his face was a palpable thing. Hot. Hard.

Her fingers flexed. And she opened her eyes wider. He was afraid. Because he could feel it too, couldn't he?

He knew that the minute they left each other and broke the spell of the ball, the magic of the mirror, washed away their surrender to the people beneath their crowns, that whatever was happening between them right here in this bed would disappear.

'Angelo—'

He dipped his head and feathered a kiss across her

forehead, the tip of her nose, then brushed his lips against hers.

'We leave now, Princess.'

Natalia watched Angelo as he stared out of the window. His body was a tight line of tension. His shoulders locked squarely. His spine was ramrod-straight.

'Stop the car here,' she said.

He raised a hand to point at the never-ending forest outside. 'We've not reached Vadelto yet.'

'It's close enough.' She unclipped her seatbelt.

He reached over. Placed his hand on top of hers and pushed the metal clip back into the hole which housed it.

'The car is still moving.'

'Make it stop,' she said. 'Please.'

He nodded.

The car halted at his command and she was unclipping, shifting over the cream leather and reaching for the handle. She pushed the door open and stepped outside.

Rain. Tiny droplets fell onto her raised face from a morning sky determined to lift the night's blanket. She closed her eyes. Stuck out her tongue.

'What are you doing?'

She opened her eyes and met his scowl of confusion. 'Living.' She smiled. *'Feeling.'*

'You'll catch a chill.' He pulled up her hood and concealed her hair, and then proceeded, wordlessly, to button her up, conceal her red-sheathed body in a long, heavy black duffel coat.

'I'm not cold,' she assured him—because she wasn't.

She was warm. Secure. Safe. Here with him. No heavy hand of protection, but a gentle reminder that he was there, protecting her. Looking after her as no one ever had. Not the Princess trapped in her palace under her father's control. But the woman.

In so many ways he'd cared for her needs. Needs she hadn't known she had. But she had them. And so did he.

'Are you coming?' she asked.

'There is nowhere to go, Princess,' he said. 'We are in no man's land here. No houses. No roads other than the one we're on.'

'Sometimes the path ahead isn't clear.' She nodded towards the treeline. 'Unless someone shows you the way.'

His eyes narrowed. 'We cannot go into the forest.'

'We can,' she said, and those butterflies gathered in her chest. 'Trust me to guide the way.'

'Trust you?' he asked.

And it rocked against her insides. All his life his brother, her...they had both gone to him to guide them. Help them. But had he ever asked for help? Ever needed it?

'Yes.' She stepped closer and took his hand. 'Trust me.'

Angelo waved off his security guards and together they entered the forest. The thick covering overhead sheltered them from the spitting rain.

The ground was damp. Soft. Their footfalls left marks on the brown earth as they swept between branches and tall trees which held no markers. No signs to her intended destination.

But she knew the way.

'How much further, Princess?' he said.

'Until we get to the top.' Her was voice high. Breathless. 'Almost there.'

The trees parted. There was a break in the covering. She pulled him through and stopped in a clearing.

'We're here.'

And there they stood. On top of *her* hill. Together. A blood-red queen with her dark king beside her.

'What do you see?' she asked, rubbing her thumb across the soft flesh between his thumb and forefinger.

He raised his free hand and swept it across the view before him. 'In front of us is your past. Your home. And beneath my feet...' He lifted a leather-clad foot and both their gazes fell. *'Leucojum vernum.* Alpine snowflakes. Common daffodils.' Angelo's gaze lifted. 'Your scent. *Spring.'*

She slipped off her hood and looked out onto the horizon. To the palace on the border.

'And behind us?' she asked.

'Camalò.'

She blew out a silent breath, but the mist leaving her lips announced it. The heaviness of it. The release of the build-up in her lungs.

'The moment I—' She swallowed. Hard. Started again. 'The moment I learnt how to escape the palace I came here.'

'To look at the view?'

'No,' she said. 'To see what was possible.'

'Possible?'

She turned. 'Change.'

His eyes flicked to the palace on the border. 'My brother?' he asked.

Natalia nodded. 'I never met him. My father did.'

The past gurgled and burst between them. A story they shared. In which they had stood on different sides of her prison bars. And yet he'd seen through them. Seen *her*. And she wanted to tell him a story too.

This story.

The story of a king who lived in a palace on the border and the Princess who had dreamed of him.

'I didn't want to meet him,' she continued, 'because at that time it never mattered to me who the man was beneath the crown—only that he would give me mine.'

'I could have been anyone,' he said, and she felt the rawness of it.

His self-rejection.

'No,' she said. 'It was always you, Angelo. It could have only ever been *you* for *me*. No one else. And I...' She swallowed. Loosened her vocal cords because she wanted her voice to be clear. Heard by his ears but felt in his chest. In his heart.

'I said I never wanted love,' she said. 'That love had no place in our marriage. Because I believed that love hurt. That it destroyed. And I believed that our duty was all that really mattered. But I was wrong. Our duty is our job. It is not who we are. You are a king. You work for your people, as I do for mine as their queen. But we are all in this together. The King. The Queen. Angelo and Natalia. You and me.'

'You are not making sense, Princess.'

'I thought love killed my mother.'

'And you no longer believe this?'

She shook her head.

'What has changed your mind?'

'Love.'

'Love?'

She nodded. 'My whole life I have thought love was to blame. For *everything*. Love killed my mother and put my father in a state of the living dead. I feared it all. My mother's love. My father's love. The power of it. The grief of it.'

'And?'

'I was wrong,' she admitted, and braced herself to reveal the organic change that had taken place over the last few weeks. The changes inside her.

'Love never kept me inside those gardens,' she continued. 'It was love that showed me the way out. The way to embrace my feelings, however new they were. However scary. I thought it was an attraction. Only something physical. Primitive. *Instinctual.*'

'That is all it was,' he said. 'All it *is.*'

He pulled away and she let him go. Let him stand in front of her. Blocking her view. Because it didn't matter. Not the palace behind her or the one in front of her. Because all she could see…all she wanted to see…was him.

And he was starting to understand.

'You're wrong,' she said hoarsely.

The heavens opened.

She laughed. Raised her face and let the heavy raindrops penetrate her skin. Clear her mind. Clarify her next steps.

She started to undo the buttons on her coat.

'What are you doing?' he rasped.

'Showing you something,' she said, and kept her eyes locked on the task at hand. Continued to release the buttons covering what it was he needed to see. So he could understand what she had only just learnt because of him. His tutelage.

'Stop it,' he demanded.

But she didn't listen. She popped the last button

and shrugged her shoulders until her ball gown came into view.

His hand halted her coat's descent and he growled, 'Put it back on.'

She raised her chin. 'No.'

'Natalia…'

'Let me show you, please,' she pleaded. 'Let go.'

The rain pelted his hair. His face. Sliding and bouncing off every sharp and contorted muscle in his face. And she understood why his hand trembled on her shoulder…because he didn't know what she was about to show him.

He was right to be scared. As she had been scared last night as she'd let love in. Discovered it.

He let go of her coat. And she let it fall. It thumped to the ground at her feet and lay with the flowers.

She raised her arms at her sides. 'What do you see?'

He raked his fingers through his hair. 'A mad queen.'

'No.' She smiled. 'Not mad. *Free.*' She dropped her hands and walked towards him. Into his space. Into *him.* 'And so are you. If you choose to be.'

'This is madness,' he said. 'You are a queen. Queens do not stand on top of a mountainous hill, performing a rain dance in a ball gown at the beginning of a storm.'

'I'm not dancing.'

'We are leaving.'

'Not yet,' she said. 'Not until you understand.'

'Understand what?'

'That we are right *here.*'

'Have you lost all sense?' he asked. 'Of course we are here. Where else would we be when you have brought us here?'

She wished she was a poet. A writer. Someone who could spin all her feelings into words he would understand. But she wasn't. She could only show him.

She grabbed his face and he didn't pull her away. But he didn't pull her into him either.

'Last night you made love to a woman. To *me*. And on my skin I can feel your kisses. I can smell your scent. Feel you inside me.' The rain fell between their lips. 'This morning we put on our clothes from the ball. Clothes that signify our jobs. Our positions. Our *duty*. But our skin beneath is still—'

She blew out an exasperated breath.

Why wasn't this easier? She knew what she meant to say and yet the words would not come.

'Our skin beneath is still what?'

'Our *skin*,' she said, because she had no better answer. 'Beneath our clothes. Beneath our titles. We are still *us*. Human beings with skin. With bones. With hearts.' And her heart thudded now. 'With names. I am Natalia. You are Angelo. And we shouldn't be fighting what and who we are.'

Her fingers pressed harder on his cheeks. She longed for his kiss. For his love. For his acceptance.

'She was a commoner, my mother. She'd never had to balance the weight of duty with her feelings, with her desires. And then she had to. And when those worlds collided she embraced all of it. All of who she was. And that is what we must do. No flames. No hiding in plain sight. No pretending we do not feel what we feel. Because we feel it. We are all things, but first we are us. We are free to choose love. To let it guide us. Shape us. Teach us.'

'Teach us what?'

'That love is a choice.' She drew closer to his mouth. Felt his hot rasps on her lips. 'And I choose you. Because—'

The butterflies gathered behind the pulsing muscle in her chest and lifted it. Pushed it free of the heavy chains that had surrounded it her entire life and opened the bars of bone.

And she gave it to him.

Her heart.

'I love you.'

And she crushed him with her love.

Her kiss.

Angelo knew he should push her away. Tear his mouth from hers and step back. Away from this wild queen saying words that made no sense. Words that had no logical meaning. Fantastical sentiments she had no right to announce. To think. *To feel*.

She had no right to make him feel.

How dared she push her lips against his so desperately and make him push back just as urgently? How dared she make him push his tongue inside her mouth as if it belonged there?

And his hands… Oh, God, his hands… They were thrusting into her hair. His fingers cradled her scalp, the bone protecting the mind that was thinking about all the wrong things. Innocent things. Sweet things.

Love?

His fingers tightened and dragged her closer. Nearer. He made her take his tongue deeper.

And, by God, it wasn't love he tasted.

It was not.

It was sex. *Lust.* Desire for the forbidden. It was who he was. A greedy man who wanted what did not belong to him.

He pulled his hands out of her wet silken locks and grabbed her elbows. And pulled. Yanked her mouth from his.

'You do not love me.'

It was a breathless roar. A growl of rejection. And it was agony. The rasp of it. The rawness of his denial. The realisation that this was the end.

The fantasy was over.

'I do.' She swiped the rain from her face. 'I love you, Angelo.'

The red fabric of her dress was transparent. Her small breasts were high, her nipples thrusting through the sodden material.

He took a step forward, and another step, until she moved backwards towards the treeline. Until the trees sheltered them both.

'You don't,' he rejected, and his chest hurt. 'You do not love me. You do not *know* me. You only know *this*—' he waved his hands to the darkening skies '—what I have allowed you to know. *Sex.*'

'It *is* love.'

'Is that why you brought us here?' He laughed. Mirthlessly. 'You thought this was what I needed?' His voice was a sneering hitch of breath. 'To be here on a mountain? So you could tell me our shared desire is love? It is not love. It is sex,' he said.

Because it was all it could be.

'And now the rain has washed away any trace,' he continued. 'Any proof that we did what we did. You are clean of me. Of the wild notion that we could bring who we were in bed into the forest. A ludicrous idea. Because it is not possible.'

'We *are* here.' Tiny beads of water trickled from the tips of her hair to roll onto her dress. The diamonds were a shiny, glittering wet mass around her hips. 'And nothing will be the same again,' she continued. '*I* will never be the same.'

'You are right,' he agreed, ignoring the fight in his body to be closer to her. To be near her. To wrap his arms around her and warm her. Shelter her from the storm. 'You will never be the same because you will never be a virgin again. You will know pleasure because I have taught you to feel it. *To want it.* I have taught you what I'm best at. Self-gratification. Regardless of the rules. Of duty. To take without thought. Without care. *I* take, Princess. With no regard to ownership. No regard to anything but the need inside me to have it. To have what I want even when it is not mine to take.'

'I gave myself to you. I am still giving myself to you. You didn't take. You didn't seek me out—not in the garden, not after we were married. I sought *you* out. The man. The King. I want them both. Angelo, I want *you*. I choose you.'

'You do not know who you are choosing.'

'Of course I do,' she said. 'You.'

'You cannot choose me because you do not know me.' He swallowed it down. The burn. The regret. He would release her. *Now.* Set her free from her illogical idealisations. 'You do not know what I have done...'

'What have you done?'

'Luciano is dead because of me,' he confessed, and whatever had been growing in his chest shrank back down into nothing but a flickering ember.

Her gaze narrowed. 'What do you mean?'

'I'm a villain, Princess. A thief. I have stolen my brother's life and I am an imposter. I'm all the bad things you've read about in your little books. I am the monster under the bed. I am what you should fear.'

'I could never fear you.'

'You should—because I've already corrupted you. I've seduced you away from your senses. From everything that mattered to you. So that I could have you. Taste you. Claim you for myself.'

'And I am claimed,' she agreed, nodding so vehemently. So agreeably. 'And I have claimed you too.'

'You are a fool.'

'*Your* fool,' she agreed.

And he scowled so hard, his face hurt.

'A fool in love,' she said.

She still didn't understand. 'I am not for loving,' he told her. 'What we have is physical. Nothing more. It can never be more.'

'Why not?' she asked, eyes as glistening as her diamond skirt. 'Maybe I'm a villain too? Because if I had to make a choice between the two—between duty or you—I would choose you. Every single time.'

No one ever chose him.

Not on purpose.

'There is only one choice, Natalia,' he hissed. 'The crown. *Our duty.* You are wrong to believe this is love. I have manipulated you. Used your naivety against you. It can never be love because my love hurts. My love kills. Didn't you hear me? It's my fault my brother is dead.'

'Yes, I heard,' she said. 'But I know he died in a fire.'

'A fire I could have prevented.'

'How?'

'I abandoned him.'

'He was a grown-up.'

'He needed me.'

'And what did *you* need?'

'To be him,' he confessed, confessing it all. 'I wanted his life. And when I knew it couldn't be mine—just as you could never be mine—when I understood how deep my desire for my brother's life went… It went bone-deep, Princess. I abandoned everything. Left him under the weight of duty. And he could not hold it up without me. The kingdom crumbled, as did he, because I took away his support.'

'Because you thought he would shine brighter without you?' she asked.

Oh, how he'd thought he'd made the right choice. Removed himself from the kingdom so his brother could be the King he'd been born to be. And he had died because of that choice.

'No, Natalia,' he rejected—because it didn't matter what he'd thought he was doing. He had been wrong to leave. To abandon him. 'I took away his only confidante. His only friend. Because I'm selfish. Because I am greedy. And I took and I took, from everything and everyone, until it bloated me. While Luciano was failing. Crumbling. *Weak*. He buckled. He died. Because of *me*.'

'But you were born the spare to the throne,' she said.

And he felt sick. Because hearing it from her mouth—the recognition of the useless entity he'd been born to be—made it all too real. The lies. The seduction.

I'm a selfish bastard.

'It was natural for you to want all the things you'd been denied in favour of the future King,' she contin-

ued. 'But you can have me now. All of me. We can have
it all. Love and duty can co-exist. We can be both King
and Queen *and* have a proper marriage where we support each other. Talk openly, as you should have with
your brother. Honestly. And we will find a solution. As
you would have with your brother, given the chance.
As maybe I would have, if I'd actually spoken to my
father and told him my true feelings, showed him what
I needed... Why didn't you tell Luciano what you were
feeling?'

'I couldn't.'

'But the lamp?'

'Was for him.'

'And the lamp was for me too, wasn't it?' she asked.
'You used it for me. To give me the release you knew
I needed.'

'No,' he said. 'This time it was for me. I needed it.
I needed—'

'Me.'

'Your body,' he corrected. 'Everything I told you last
night was a lie. A fantasy. A twisted tale told to seduce.
To captivate. To corrupt. Because I have always wanted
you. Desired you. Because it is in my nature to want
what is not mine. To crave what is forbidden. And now
I've had you—'

'Don't,' she interrupted, her nostrils flaring as rapidly as her chest. 'Angelo—'

She reached for him and he grasped her wrist. Held
it and made his body be still. Not react. He dropped it
and she let her arm fall to her side.

'Hear this, Princess,' he said, with all the command
of the King. The imposter King that he was, whom all
would now obey. Including her. Including himself. He

would make it so. 'There was only ever one choice. *Duty*. You might already carry my heir,' he announced.

And he wanted to fall to his knees and place his cheek on her stomach. To hold her as she cradled his head, the bones that housed his mind, which was screaming at him not to do this.

But he wouldn't listen.

Because for one night he'd let himself be the man he truly was. *Greedy*. And if he stayed with her he would suck the life out of her the way he had with Luciano.

'The deed is done,' he finished. And his flesh tightened. Squeezed. Until everything hurt. His head. His body. His bones. 'And now we will co-exist. Separately.'

Something inside him tore.

'Separately?' she said.

He nodded. Because he was done. All out of words. He'd told her what he'd done to Luciano and how he'd tricked her. Manipulated her for his own greed. His selfish needs. And still she would not run.

'Duty tethers us,' he reminded her. Himself. It was what they were. All they could ever be. 'And our duty we will do—because we must. But everything else...'

'Everything else?'

'Never existed.'

'But I hurt...'

'You do not know pain,' he growled from deep in his chest. 'I have hurt for so long I do not know what it is to *not* feel pain. I am agony personified because of *you*. If I had never wanted you, Luciano would be alive.'

Her face fell. Blanched. 'You blame *me*?'

'You are my weakness and I must cut you out. I must end this.'

'Wait...'

His body hardened. And he didn't know why he waited, but he did. He waited for her anger, for tears, for disappointment. But none of it was there.

She stood taller, angled her chin. Her hands, so still, sat at her sides. A queen.

'If you need space—'

'This is not about time apart.'

She ignored him.

'In the last twenty-four hours we have covered a lot of ground. Spoken about so much and yet so little. It is not my fault your brother is dead. But this isn't about me.'

'It was always about you.'

'Was it?' she asked. 'Was it about me? Or has it firmly been about you? Denying everything you could have had if only you'd used your words and asked for what you needed. You said I kept myself in the dark. But I think—*no, I know*,' she corrected, 'that you have kept yourself in the dark too. In the shadows all your life. But right now,' she continued hurriedly, 'I want you to know that I am listening to what *you* need. And I will wait—'

'I will not come.'

He wouldn't.

'I will wait,' she said again. 'For you.'

His heart pumped. *Hard.* He'd dragged her into his fantasy. Into his twisted world of greed. And now he almost believed it was true. That this was real. That *they* could be real.

But it wasn't real.

It was a lie.

'I am going to walk away,' he said, and readied himself for the final blow that would end everything between them. 'And you will go back to Vadelto with my men. You will not come back until you are summoned... until you are needed. You will not come to me because I will never call your name. *I* will never summon you. Never for myself. Because I do not want you any more. I have had you. And I am done with you.'

An image of his father flashed in his mind.

He had used the pretty thing and now he would discard it.

For Luciano.

For the kingdom.

For *her*.

'Goodbye, Natalia.'

He turned his back. And despite himself he listened for his name with every step he took away from her. His body stiffened. His joints protested with every step, wanting him to turn back. To get on his knees and—

And what?

He could not love her.

He could not let her love him.

But he hurt. And the pain was a war inside him. A battle he'd already lost three years ago. He would not drag her down with him. He would not ruin her any more than he already had. He would save her the only way he knew how.

By letting her go.

CHAPTER ELEVEN

Two weeks later...

THE DOOR WAS rapped upon consecutively three times.

'Natalia?'

Her father.

She groaned inwardly and punched a pillow. 'Go away,' she muttered, and rolled on to her stomach. Buried her face into feathers that seemed to bear a permanent imprint of her skull.

The door opened anyway.

She groaned louder, turned and sat up.

'Father,' she acknowledged—because there he stood, at the end of her bed.

She couldn't visualise another time when her father had ever been in her rooms. Not to tell her a story. Not to kiss her goodnight. Not for anything. But here he was.

Her father moved towards her, around the side of the bed, and held out an envelope.

'What is it?'

She took it. Ran her hands over the smooth, unmarked front. Her chest twitched. Her ears pricked. And she knew what it was loosening the tightness in her chest. She almost dared not name it. Recognise it. Because every day she had waited for him. For a sign. And every day he hadn't come.

But she couldn't ignore the flicker in her chest.

Hope.

Eyes so similar to hers narrowed. 'You are to be ready at six,' her father said.

She frowned. 'For what?'

She tore the envelope open, pulled free a gold-embossed invitation addressed to King Angelo and Queen Natalia for an engagement celebration.

He'd summoned her.

For duty.

He wasn't coming. He was never coming to summon her. He wanted only a queen, and any queen would do.

Never *her*. Never this woman he'd freed and taught how to feel however big her emotions were. And she couldn't cage her. Didn't know how to put on her crown and face him as she had all those weeks ago. Ready and certain of her future. Her destiny.

Her breath caught.

She was as alone as she'd ever been.

'Tell the King I'm not well,' she said, because she didn't feel well. Her body was weak. Her brain sluggish.

'And what is this sickness that keeps you in bed?' her father asked. 'What invisible illness has kept you away from your people—away from me—for two weeks?'

Natalia didn't know what instinct to react to first. Her instinct to smooth her rumpled hair, or her instinct to apologise for not seeking him out on her return and explaining her presence.

It had been so easy to slide back into her old life. Her old rooms. Her old bed.

She hadn't known what to tell him.

She still didn't.

So she didn't do or say anything. She just sat there, in the middle of her bed, at nearly noon, and looked at him.

Her father.

A man she didn't really know.

A man who had tried to keep her safe from harm by keeping them all locked inside a time warp.

But wasn't she doing the same now? She'd climbed into the familiar and stayed there.

Her father couldn't protect her now.

Not him, nor those guards standing in every corridor, in front of every door, nor the secretly armed guards in the shadows.

It was too late to save her from the danger she'd never recognised.

With open arms she'd thrown herself in danger's way and it had consumed her. Eaten her alive and spat her out. Raw, but brand-new.

Changed.

And she didn't know how to stop it. How to turn back time and take it back. Make it go away.

All these things inside her had no way out without a guide to direct her. A teacher to awaken her to the technique to harness it. It was just *there*. All the time. A need. A want.

But there was nothing to have.

She hated herself.

She was the antithesis of everything she had ever hoped to become.

Consumed by a nonsensical feeling.

An *unrequited* feeling.

She laughed. A strange noise. A moan, a sob, a wail…all combined in a few hiccups of sound.

'What is funny?' her father asked.

She met his gaze squarely. Lifted her chin. 'I've just realised what's wrong with me.'

'Do you require a doctor?'

She shook her head.

'So what is it?' Eyes wide, he pushed. 'What is this mysterious illness that has caused you to abandon your king and your people?'

She willed her lips to move, to smile, but she couldn't find the will to lie, to ignore the truth that was confining her to bed.

So she told him the truth.

'My heart is broken.'

She sniffed. Her nose felt blocked. Her throat was sore. But it was heartbreak, wasn't it?

Angelo had broken her heart and left her bleeding. An invisible wound she didn't know how to heal. Nor would any doctor.

'Then mend it,' her father growled. 'Get out of bed, get dressed, and remember who you are.'

Her heart thudded weakly. 'And who am I?'

'A daughter who will do her duty.'

Maybe Angelo was right. Maybe there was no room in royal life for anything but what others needed them to be.

She wasn't allowed to feel this, was she? She wasn't allowed to be human and stay in bed? To be sad? To have emotions?

She was the Queen.

But she *was* sad.

Because something that had felt so close, so attainable, had been ripped from her exposed and trembling hands and crushed before her very eyes. Stamped into the soil. Buried deep beneath the earth. Until there were no visible signs any more. Only his retreating form. His rigid shoulders. Leaving her behind with only sorrow.

This impenetrable sadness.

Was this grief? This tightness in her chest? This heavy weight in her gut? This mass that expanded every day, making it difficult to breathe? To think?

Was she grieving?

Was this the kind of queen Natalia wanted to be? Frozen. Suspended in time. Lost in a moment.

Had she become her father?

She looked at him. At a man who had loved and lost. Because of *her*.

'Is *your* heart still broken?' she asked.

Because she wanted to know if this pain had an end. She wanted to know if in these last twenty-one years while he'd sat with his grief he'd become comfortable with it. Was it bearable now? Or—

'It is, isn't it?' she said, without giving him a chance to respond.

Her father's mouth compressed. His eyes stared at her. Hard.

'I understand now,' she said. Because how could her father be anything other than what he had always been to her all these years? A father who had to love her from a distance because the pain was too sharp, too visceral, when he got too close to her. She was the only living reminder of everything that was dead. *Gone.*

'How do you understand?' he asked.

'Because I feel the same,' she replied.

'Feel what?'

'A never-ending grief for what I've lost.'

'What have you lost?'

'Angelo.'

It was ridiculous, wasn't it? She was sad about the loss of a love that had never been hers to claim. He hadn't ever wanted her.

But she'd lost love anyway, hadn't she? Lost him. She'd pushed him too hard and too fast, trying to make him understand a feeling she barely understood herself. But she knew it. Recognised it. Felt it. On her skin. In her bones.

In her heart.

'And,' she continued, 'I don't know how I will put on my crown and stand at his side and pretend what happened between us never existed. When he will be right there beside me. When I will have to look at him, knowing we could be so much more. We could have it all. But he doesn't want it. *None of it.* Nothing of what I offer as myself.'

'How dare you?' Colour flared in her father's cheeks. 'How dare you compare *my* pain to your childish reaction to something that has happened between you and Angelo? *He* is alive.'

'I—'

'Your mother is dead.'

'Do you think I don't know that?' she croaked. 'I know that every day I remind you of what I took from you. My mother. Your love. How could your heart ever heal when you had to look at me every day? The daughter who took it all from you?'

A pulse flickered in his jaw. 'Is that what you think?'

She sighed. 'It's what I *know*.'

'And what have I done to make you think I can't bear to look at you?' he said. 'I have *always* looked at you. I *am* looking. You are my daughter.'

She swallowed down old hurts and made herself respond. Truthfully. Because what was the point in holding back?

'Exactly,' she agreed. 'But I am my mother's daughter too, aren't I?' Her cheeks grew hot. 'You loved her and I took her from you. And you responded accordingly, didn't you?'

'How did I respond?'

'The only way you could,' she said, and wiped an open palm over her burning eyes. 'You did your duty. You protected me from harm. Made sure I was fed. I was clothed. Educated. Prepared for the world of being a princess. A queen. I know how to dance, how to smile, how to converse and charm. But I do not know—' she met his eyes squarely...lifted her chin '—how to love. How to cope with the loss of love. I only know how to do what I saw *you* do.'

'What *did* I do?'

'Grieve,' she said. 'Desperately and devoutly.'

He closed his eyes, and Natalia watched a thousand emotions she couldn't name flit across his face.

And then she saw it. *Felt* it.

'Regret,' she whispered, acknowledging it to herself. 'I'm your biggest regret, aren't I?'

'I do not regret a moment with your mother. Or the choices we made together. I do not regret—' he opened his eyes '—you.'

'How can you not?' she croaked. 'When every day I remind you of her? When every decision you've ever made about me—about Vadelto—was because—'

'I was scared,' he finished for her.

Pain was etched in his every muscle. And she knew this pain. How hard his confession was to voice. Because she was scared too. Of life. Of loving. Of losing love and carrying on as if it had never happened. When it *had* happened. To her.

Love.

Everything she'd ever feared. The consuming nature of it. The grief of it. The power it had to bring her to her knees and make her forget everything else.

'And I am so sorry,' her father continued. 'Sorry I protected you so harshly...guarded you from the world. But I couldn't lose you. Couldn't stand the idea or the possibility that you'd be taken from me too. I see my mistake now.'

'What mistake?' she breathed.

'I thought I was protecting you.' He swallowed thickly. 'But I was failing you.'

'How?'

'I prepared you for everything,' he answered. 'Everything but life. Not for living it. Not for love. And here you are, defenceless against it. Against love. The pain of it.'

'I don't feel defenceless. I feel raw. Exposed. But...' She shrugged. 'I'm grateful.'

'Grateful?'

'Yes,' she acknowledged—to him...to herself. 'Angelo changed me. I *am* changed. And, regardless of what I feel now, in the future I know it will make me stronger. I will be a better queen for having lived a life. Even if it was only for a moment. A truthful, undeniable moment of living. The excitement of possibility. I have tasted it. *Felt* it. Like my mother.'

'Your mother?' he repeated, his voice thick with emotion.

She smiled. Tentatively. 'She was clever, wasn't she?' she asked. 'Brave?'

'Was she?'

'Yes.'

'Why?'

'Because she lived, didn't she? Fearlessly. Pushed life to its limits even when she knew the risks of her pregnancy. The risk of giving birth to me.'

She swallowed down the lump in her throat. Made herself clarify her thoughts. Her feelings. Her understanding of what she now understood.

'You couldn't stop her, could you?' she asked. 'You couldn't make her rest when all she wanted to do was live. You didn't want to stop her because you loved her. Supported her dreams as she supported yours.'

'She was a light,' he said roughly. 'She pulled everything and everyone into her warmth with her effortless charm...her zest to make things better with just a little more here, a little more there.' His nostrils flared. 'I thought she was immortal. A goddess given to me by some divine entity. I never considered all the risks. That she was mortal, like me. Because she was everything I wasn't. She was hope. She was life. She was my love.'

'And when she died it reminded you of your own mortality?' she asked. 'Of mine?'

Jaw set, he nodded. 'But you gave me life, Natalia. A reason to live when I thought I had none. You're a part of me as much as you are a part of your mother. You are the proof of our love. The legacy of it. And I would do it all again. Love her despite the pain. Because she was a gift. *Love* is a gift.'

'Angelo doesn't love me.'

The dam almost broke then. She hid behind her hands, stemmed the tears, halted them in their tracks.

Arms...the strong arms she'd always known would keep her safe...wrapped around her and drew her in. A sob burst from her lips. One tear fell, and then the next, and they kept coming.

'You don't have to go tonight,' he assured her, and relief flooded through her.

'Thank you,' she said.

Because she wasn't ready. Not yet. Duty could wait. She needed time, didn't she? *More time.* To heal. To build up walls around herself and look at him as a king. Any king. Not *her* king.

She needed to experience this. Harden herself to it. And then she would face him without regret, but with acceptance. *This* was what he needed. What he wanted.

A queen.

Only a queen.

'Take all the time you need, Natalia,' her father said against her head.

And she relaxed into his hold. Accepted his love for what it was. And how he could give it to her. The only way he could allow himself to love his daughter. With distance. With logic. With pain.

And she would teach herself to love Angelo this way too.

She wasn't coming.

Angelo had readied himself for everything but that.

He didn't know what to do. With his face. His hands. His feet refused to push him forward, to step outside and get him into the waiting helicopter. His mind had paused. The synapses in his brain refused to fire. To connect. To join the dots.

'What do you mean, she isn't coming?'

His throat pushed out the words and his mouth spoke them, but it was not his voice. It was a rumble of the roar that was getting bigger in his chest.

A muscle in his jaw pulsed. He felt it. The deep thrum of emotion. Of feelings he'd sworn to bury deeper. He'd promised to lock them away and never consider them again. Forget them the way he'd forgotten her.

Forgotten her? Liar!

It had been agony.

He'd wanted to climb into her bed and refuse to get out. Push his face into her pillow. Bury his nose until the feathers pushed into his skin. Until all he could taste—all he could inhale—was her.

But he had resisted the urge to soothe himself. To be close to her and her fading scent. Because he didn't deserve to be soothed. He deserved to hurt. To be in pain. Because he'd hurt her. *Knowingly.*

'Your Majesty—' The aide swallowed thickly, cast his eyes down and bent his head. Bowing in an apology that was not his to give. 'The Vadelton palace apologises. The Queen is unwell.'

'Unwell?' he asked—not a rumble, not a roar, but an anguished yelp.

'The Queen is suffering from a common cold,' the aide answered, without raising his head.

Angelo turned rigid. *A common cold?* He'd had several colds throughout his lifetime and never had they prevented him from doing his duty. From answering any royal summons. And yet she had refused his. Refused to attend when duty demanded that she did.

What was he supposed to do? Collect her? Demand she face his duty, as he was? Hand her a tissue?

Jaw clenched, he stood there. Motionless. Overwrought with...nothing.

Was this a power move? A manipulative choice to bring him to her? To make *him* come to *her* when he'd sworn he wouldn't? Not Angelo. Not the man she'd claimed to—

He closed his eyes. She would never do that. Manipulate him for her own gains. That was *him*. The manipulator. The liar. Not Natalia. Not the woman or the Queen.

And how do you know that? Because you know her?

Maybe. But most of all he knew what he'd done. Revealed himself to her. All the ugly parts.

And despite what she'd said—her promise that she would wait—he knew that time often clarified what even the most innocent didn't want to understand.

The sensations of their night together would have dulled. Blurred. However competent his seduction, time away from him, from the chemistry that burned between them, would have given her nothing but the bold strokes of the truth.

The truth of him.

He was a usurper.

An imposter.

A crown-stealer.

It wasn't a power move...but it was a move, wasn't it?

She'd changed her mind. Her waiting was over. *They* were over. She didn't want him. Not the man she now knew he was. Because that man was a lie. A trick. A tease. He'd tricked her. Made her think she could lean on him and he'd support her.

Now she understood the truth.

She needed no one but herself.

Angelo opened his eyes, and who knew what the aide saw in his unseeing stare? Because he vanished. Moved with speed as if he'd never been there.

The path ahead was clear.

Angelo put one foot in front of the other and prepared to do the only thing he could.

He'd take the forty-minute helicopter ride. Fly over the alpine kingdom of snow-peaked mountains and across a violet-streaked sky to the small kingdom of Tinto. A country of only fifteen hundred people, nestled deep in the Alps. He'd nod his head accordingly. Celebrate the engagement of their king to their new queen-in-waiting with an appropriately sized smile.

Alone.

He ignored the stumble of his feet as he got into the helicopter. The ground must be uneven. He was fine. And most of all he knew she would be fine.

This was how it had always been meant to be.

The party was in full swing. A room full of people wagged their tongues with raised champagne flutes.

Angelo was done. He'd greeted and congratulated and now he withdrew. Not from the room, with its low-hanging chandeliers and glittering ball gowns, but into himself. And he stayed there. Behind his crown. His duty. And he watched them. Strangers bound by their elite status. Their place in the world.

Politically, this engagement meant nothing to him.

Natalia's absence would not be noted. People got ill. It was forgivable.

But *he* noticed.

He was aware of an absence at his side, as if she were a missing limb. His right hand. His dominant hand. His left hand was useable. It sufficed. But it did not feel like the right one. Did not hold steady. *Strong.* It was only there. As he was. Here and yet not here. Imbalanced.

He flexed his fingers, imagined her tiny fingers in his. Holding his hand not because duty demanded she did, but because she wanted to.

He crushed his hands into fists and ended the tingling in his palms.

He would forget.

He would make himself forget.

She didn't want him. And the only thing he should feel was relief.

She was free of him. The weight of him. It was a pressure that would have suffocated her. His selfishness would have pressed against her young lungs until she couldn't draw breath.

He would not close his eyes. He would not allow himself to withdraw deeper into his thoughts. Thoughts of her. How different tonight could have been if she was here.

She wasn't here.

Angelo's breath halted. He saw him before he'd been seen. The old King cut through the dance floor, and as if they could sense his power the people parted to allow him through.

Green eyes so like Natalia's zeroed in on him. He moved with the long strides of a man confident of his destination. Him. The son-in-law he'd given his daughter to.

The wrong son.

The wrong king.

Angelo sat rigid in his seat. The memory triggered in his mind was clear and vivid. A party in a penthouse suite in London. A man who had not belonged there crossing a room to get to him, drunk on a sofa. He had whispered in his ear. A hiss of low breath. Words he would never forget.

An unwavering soberness had followed those words. The punch of them. The King was dead. His brother was gone...

With open palms spread on his thighs beneath the circular table, empty but for the crystal glasses and silver spoons left by its departed guests, Angelo stood.

He braced his shoulders. Planted his feet. But he could not stem the trembling in his core. And it spread. A weakness. Fatiguing his every limb. His every muscle.

The old King approached, and Angelo's chest heaved. But he could not speak. Could not will his mouth to ask the question. Because he did not want to hear the answer. He did not want the hiss of breath, the words he knew wouldn't give him sobriety.

They would end him.

He'd done it again.

She was—

'No.'

The word shuddered from his lips in a plea. He was begging the old King not to do it. Not to tell him. Not to whisper in his ear.

A cold? It had never been a cold, had it? It was a sickness. A sickness he could have prevented if he'd never agreed to follow her into the forest. If the rain had not soaked her pale, delicate flesh. The cold had got inside her. Into her body. Her lungs. He'd failed to protect her. He'd let it happen.

Again.

He closed his eyes. And there she was. Where she had always been. Inside him.

Natalia.

His bold queen. Holding his hand. Giving him everything he'd never thought he deserved. Support.

Love.

'Son?' A hand touched his shoulder. 'Are you all right?'

He opened his eyes and met the old King's.

'Is she…?' It was a croak. A question pulled from the depths of his subconscious that needed words. He needed to know.

The King shook his head. 'No.'

Angelo's knees buckled. 'No…?'

'She is heartbroken.'

Heartbroken?

'She's alive?'

Everything stopped. Waited. Hinged on his reply.

The old King scowled. 'Of course she is.'

And Angelo fell.

His knees gave way.

But the old King caught him by the elbow with a firm grip, directed him into the vacated seat behind him and sat down beside him.

Neither spoke. They just sat beside each other with unseeing eyes and thudding hearts.

'I thought…' Angelo swallowed. Cleared his throat. 'The palace said she was unwell.'

'She is,' the old King agreed.

'A cold?' Angelo rasped.

'No, not a cold,' the old King said.

He was oblivious to the pain of the lies he'd told to the palace. A lie that had made Angelo think the worst. Made him feel the loss of it. Of her. The Princess who never should have been his.

But, by God, he wanted her. *Here.* To touch her. Hold her. Whisper in her ear words he'd thought he never would.

Words of a man. Not a king.

Words shared between lovers.

Words of devotion.

Of—

'Tell me,' the old King said, 'what do you see?'

He waved an open palm towards the dance floor, towards guests who were not looking at a former king and his son-in-law exchanging words. They were oblivious to everything but themselves and who they were wagging their own tongues with.

What *did* he see?

'Duty,' Angelo answered—because that was what he saw.

'A lie,' the old King rejected. 'A falsity. A charade. The people in this room want recognition for their riches. Recognition for how high they stand in a world full of powerful men. They want recognition for things that don't matter, because they have forgotten what does.'

'What does matter?'

'People.'

'Are they not people?'

'Yes, but they have forgotten what that means.'

'What does it mean?'

'Many think my country is backward,' he replied. 'And in many ways it is. I understand what my wife wanted to do, and what Natalia intends to continue. But my country is strong because the people understand what matters. What is important.'

'What is it?' Angelo asked. 'What's important?'

'Love.'

Angelo's chest ached. *Intensely.*

'Love?'

'For the person standing beside you,' he said.

'I don't understand,' Angelo admitted. His mind was jarred. His thinking process stunted.

'This room is full of people who believe they know what it means to be king. It overshadows the truth of what it means to rule well. My people understand the importance of pushing through every day because of the person beside them. For the people they love. Because that is all they have. The world is not watching them. No one is applauding them. It is only them. And it was only us. It was only me and my daughter. And she gave me the strength to remember that all this—' he waved to the room again '—is nothing more than a prop for an oversized ego.'

Angelo inhaled deeply, blowing his breath out silently between pursed lips. 'And that is why you closed Valdeto's borders?'

The old King nodded. A single dip of confirmation. 'When my wife died, I needed to be reminded. People come before anything else. People are the foundation of what makes us strong. My daughter had to come first. Natalia gave me the strength to carry on when I didn't think I could. Everything I have done, I have done for her. To keep her close. To make her strong. A woman who does not need all *this*.'

Angelo looked around at the opulence. The grandeur. What did it really mean? Did it clothe and feed the people? Did it nourish their spirits? This charade of duty?

Duty had broken them all, hadn't it?

His father, in his need to be the best, the strongest, had produced two broken sons. His mother had abandoned her children because of it—this duty that had crushed and killed his twin.

He hadn't killed him, had he?

Duty had.

Because they'd all forgotten what it meant to be human. How to do what they did for each other.

'And yet she is undone,' the old King continued.

'Undone?' Angelo said huskily.

'I kept her too close and yet too far away.' The old King shook his head. 'And all I have tried to teach her is unravelling, because she does not understand the power she has found.'

'Power?'

'To be human.' He swallowed thickly. 'To love. And I love my daughter.'

Natalia's father turned and held Angelo's gaze.

'Do *you*?'

CHAPTER TWELVE

NATALIA HEARD THE chopper overhead but ignored it. Her father was the only one who used it and he did so often.

The high, full moon illuminated the garden in a soft white light. She fingered the climbing vines and walked forward, through the walls of tall bushes she'd always thought were keeping her inside, imprisoning her in their never-ending maze.

Angelo had thought she was a prisoner, too.

She remembered now. His story. A story told by a king of when he had been a prince and his queen had been a princess.

They'd both been prisoners, hadn't they? Because they hadn't met. Hadn't taught each other what it meant to be free. To feel. To love.

She loved him. Knew it. Felt it. But he was still a prisoner. A prisoner of pain and rejection. *Self-rejection.* Because he'd never believed he was worthy of love as himself. *For* himself.

She dropped her hands to her sides. Closed her eyes. Raised her face to the moon. She understood that she was worthy now. Worthy of her father's love. Her *own* love. She was allowed and entitled to love herself. She was the person she had to look at in the mirror. And after all this time she liked the woman reflected back at her. A woman who could feel, however much it hurt.

She was alive, she was breathing, and she was right here. Feeling. Loving. *Living.* But she understood what she hadn't before. What she had tried and failed to do on top of that mountain.

She couldn't teach Angelo to love himself, however hard she loved him. But she could show him every day that she loved him. When she returned to the palace she would hold his hand. No grand proclamations of love, because he wasn't ready. She understood that now— just as he had understood that she hadn't been ready to welcome him into her bedroom the night he'd kissed her as no other had.

Feelings grew, and as they did you needed space to get to know them. To get comfortable with them. As she had these last two weeks. She had been getting comfortable with her pain. Her love. Trying to understand what she needed to do with those feelings. She wouldn't cage them. Wouldn't ignore them. Because life was to feel, wasn't it?

She'd give him time. Because those changes were already happening inside him. Organic changes she couldn't force.

She would wait.

The sound of metal on metal pierced the silence.

Her eyes flew open. Her head turned.

Angelo.

Dishevelled. His hair swished in all directions. His bow tie hung undone beside the collar of his open-collared shirt. And his face… Oh, his beautiful face. It was contorted into harsh lines of yearning.

She felt it. The need to be closer. To touch this apparition standing in the moonlight.

Her urge was to run. To fling her arms around his neck and rain kisses on his face. But she didn't. She stood rooted. And waited.

Slowly…painfully slowly…he moved closer. His eyes were on her and hers were on him until he stood before her.

Desperately, she wanted to place an open palm on his cheek. But how could she reach out and touch him when he wasn't ready to feel? To understand the feeling she embraced him with?

Love.

And despite her pep talk, her willingness to wait for him to be ready, *she* wasn't ready. She wasn't ready to touch him without loving him openly…with words, with kisses.

She closed her eyes.

Warmth. She felt it at the side of her cheek. Not the touch of him, but the hesitation before it. And she wanted to end his hesitation, place her hand on top of his and push it down. On to her cheek. Her skin.

She didn't. She opened her eyes and met his. Her question was in them.

Why was he here?

She stepped back. His hand fell. His jaw locked.

He needed a queen. That was all. And that was what she'd give him.

'How was the party?'

His lips twisted. 'Party?'

'Tonight,' she said. 'The event.' She raised her chin. 'I'll be ready for the next one. There's no need for you to come here. I know what I need to do. What you need me to be.'

'What I need you to be?' he repeated, and his voice was a broken husk.

Everything in her hurt, because she couldn't draw him to her. End this agony for both of them.

He wasn't ready.

'A queen,' she said, standing tall, just as he needed her to. Standing above her feelings, her emotions. Putting her crown before it all.

'That isn't what I need.'

He fell to his knees.

She reached for him to pull him up. 'Angelo—'

'No!'

He closed his eyes, and a thousand emotions she couldn't name flashed across every chiselled plane of his face. His hands moved, reached for the open neck of his shirt and tugged. Each black pearl-shaped button popped. He tore free the shirt from his sliver buckled belt, from his trousers, to reveal the hard muscles of his abdomen.

She trembled.

His head rose. Dark eyes seeking and capturing hers. 'What do you see?'

'Your chest.'

'What else?'

'Your skin.'

'And what is beneath my skin, Princess?'

The mountain. It flashed into her mind. Leading him through the thick forest to the place where she had dreamed a dream of him.

Dared she think it?

Dared she believe he understood what she could not find the words for?

Her heart thudding, she answered, 'You.'

He shook his head. Placed his flat, open palm to the middle of his chest. 'My heart.'

'Your heart?'

He nodded. 'Tonight, I thought I'd lost it. The reason my heart beats. *Who* it beats for.'

'I don't understand…'

'You are my heart, Natalia,' he said, and her own heart soared.

But she pushed it down, closed the cage. Because what if she was wrong? What if this wasn't what she thought was?

'What—'

'I am not finished. I always thought my reason for being on this earth was to fulfil my duty. To my father. My brother.' His chest heaved. 'And when I could no longer do my duty I ran away. I forgot—maybe I never knew—why I should have stayed.'

'Why should you have stayed?' she pushed.

'For love.'

'Love?'

'I loved my brother. But I forgot about that love. The love that bound us together. And I craved all the things that did not matter. The power of a king. But here I am a king. *Powerless*.'

'Powerless?' she repeated.

He didn't look powerless. He was the definition of strong vulnerability. Showing a raw, unguarded moment of honesty. And she had never loved him more than she did in this moment.

His chest was exposed. His heart was breaking free to the surface.

Was he going to give it to her?

'Yes, powerless,' he said. 'I thought because I wanted you, that meant I wanted it all. My brother's life. And here I am, living a life that never should have been mine. I have it all. But all I still want—all I need—is you. Because I love you.'

'You love me?'

'I have been in love with you since the moment I saw you in these gardens. My heart knew before my brain could decipher it. This knowing…this recognition… this *love* has always been between us. Without instigation. Without reason. It was just always there. Will *always* be there.'

It was poetry.

It was everything she hadn't been able to put into words.

It was love.

'I'm sorry,' he said. 'I am sorry I hurt you. I am sorry I pushed you away so violently. I was vile. I was cruel. And that is not the man I want to be. That was a disguise. I was hiding behind it because I was—'

'Scared,' she finished for him. 'Hurting.'

'That's no excuse,' he rasped. 'I am sorry.'

'I forgive you,' she whispered hoarsely. 'Now you need to forgive yourself. For everything. For Luciano. It wasn't your fault. Just as the death of my mother wasn't mine. They lived their own lives. Made their own choices. Now we must make choices for ourselves, too.'

'I…'

'I don't need any more words. I don't need you to

talk if you're not ready. You don't need to say anything. Because I know what matters.'

'What do you know, Natalia?'

His chest heaved. And suddenly she couldn't stand it. This distance between them. So she got down on her knees too and cupped his beautiful face.

'You love me,' she answered. 'You have always loved me.'

He dipped his head until their foreheads met. 'It's true.'

'I know.'

'I am ready,' he said. 'Ready to talk.'

'And I will listen,' she promised. 'Every day for the rest of our lives. I will hear you. See you. Whether we are in the royal spotlight or behind it I will hold your hand.'

She placed her hand on top of his. On his chest. On his heart.

'And I will hold yours,' he growled. 'Because it was always you for me. I was a coward. I feared what doors would open if I told Luciano the truth of what I was feeling. If I told you… And now I realise if I had opened my mouth, talked honestly—'

'We can't change the past,' she said, wanting to ease the pain she could feel in him. His regret for his brother. 'But we can accept it. Start again. Make different choices. Better choices. Because together we are stronger. Stronger in our love.'

'Our love,' he agreed. 'I love you. Everything about you. I need you, Natalia. To guide me. Teach me. Be with me. Always.'

'Always,' she promised.
He nodded. 'This time, we choose each other.'
'We choose love.'

EPILOGUE

Five years later...

THE BLACK ROLLS-ROYCE moved through the golden gates with slow precision into the forecourt of the mountain-side train station.

The crowd roared, and in their hands they waved tiny flags of deep blues and bold reds. Neither Camalò's flag nor Vadelto's, but a new flag, made up of the combined colours of two nations once separated by a border and a king's grief.

But they were one entity now. One kingdom. One heart. Joined and strengthened by love. A king's love for his queen and hers for him.

Natalia's heart was full. Full of pride and love for a journey that had come full circle to her mountain. To her hill. Where a princess had dreamed of a brighter future. Of change. Of a king who would gift it all to her.

And he had.

Beside her sat her king, her husband, her Angelo. He was the never-ending source of strength she'd never expected, as she was for him. In or out of the royal spotlight, they held each other's hand. As they did now.

'Is it everything you hoped for, Princess?'

'It is.'

She turned. Met a gaze that held hers with love. A love that was as clear as the bump swelling her stomach beneath the silver gown. She placed her hand on it. On the proof of their love, the legacy of it, growing inside her.

'And so much more.'

His eyes flashed and she burnt. As she always did. For his touch. For him. *Only him.*

His big hand splayed over hers on her stomach. 'I'm so glad we waited,' he said rawly. 'Waited until now to have our children.' Dark eyebrows rose high above wide eyes. '*Twins*... Twins who will know the unconditional love we share for each other and for them. Twins who will be known for themselves. Who—' He swallowed thickly.

Natalia placed her free hand on his cheek. 'I know,' she soothed—because she did.

She knew him as well as she knew herself. Together, they had revisited old hurts and put them to rest. She understood that didn't mean they didn't hurt any more, nor did regrets vanish because they had talked about them honestly.

But she knew that together they shared each other's burdens, lightened the load for each other. They challenged each other to think, to talk, and they decided together how the future would be different. Better. *Stronger.*

Because together they were strong. A team. A husband and wife. A king and queen who had changed the entire infrastructure of their kingdoms and brought untold prosperity.

He closed his eyes, dipped his chin, and kissed the

underside of her wrist. 'I love you, Natalia Dizieno. So very much.'

She smiled. 'I know.'

And she did. Because every day for the last five years he had shown her just how much.

Behind closed doors they were a never-ending fire of desire, but they also had a slow-burning intimacy. They had chats over fireside picnics, where there was always something new to discover about each other, a different story to tell. And fresh stories too. Stories they had created together.

He opened his eyes. 'I'm so very proud of you,' he said, beaming with the truth of his statement. 'This—' He waved towards the window. To the crowds on either side of the barrier and the red carpet leading to a podium on the railway platform. 'All this would never have been possible without you.'

'That's not true,' she said. 'Teams work together. They talk, they come up with shared ideas, and together they make them bigger. Better. *Stronger*.'

'I never would have thought of trains.'

She grinned. 'Ideas are simple. Executing them is the hard part. And without you we wouldn't be about to open our very first railway.'

It was a magnificent railway. It spanned the mountains themselves, moved over hillsides and travelled through Vadelton villages. It stopped at the educational institutes that had been built and blossomed in the last five years, and other tourist spots besides.

It was a railway for their people. For pleasure. For work. But it would also be a tourist attraction. A sleeper train that would take its passengers on adventures only their new alpine kingdom could provide.

But *this* train was theirs.

Tonight, the King and Queen would take its maiden voyage. An eight-hour adventure of scenic views, complemented by good food on their plates and exceptional company at their sides.

Just them.

And together, tonight, they would celebrate five years of change. Some organic and some, like her railway, a dream she had fantasised over turned real.

As they were.

A dream come true.

* * * * *

Were you blown away by
The King She Shouldn't Crave?
Then jump headfirst into these other
Lela May Wight stories!

His Desert Bride by Demand
Bound by a Sicilian Secret

Available now!

#4185 THE SECRET OF THEIR BILLION-DOLLAR BABY
Bound by a Surrogate Baby
by Dani Collins

Sasha married billionaire Rafael Zamos to escape her stepfather's control. But is the gilded cage of her convenient union any better? Lost within their marital facade, Sasha fiercely protects her heart while surrendering to her husband's intoxicating touch... Might a child bring them closer?

#4186 THE KING'S HIDDEN HEIR
by Sharon Kendrick

Emerald Baker was a cloakroom attendant when she spent one mind-blowing night with a prince. Now Konstandin is a king—and he insists that Emmy marry him when she tells him he is a father! For the sake of her son, she'll consider his ruthlessly convenient proposal...

#4187 A TYCOON TOO WILD TO WED
The Teras Wedding Challenge
by Caitlin Crews

All innocent Brita Martis craves is freedom from her grasping family, and marrying powerful Asterion Teras may be her best chance of escape. The chemistry that burns between them at first sight thrills her, but when their passion explodes, she is lost! Unless she can tame the wildest tycoon of all...

#4188 TWIN CONSEQUENCES OF THAT NIGHT
by Pippa Roscoe

When billionaire Nate Harcourt jets to Spain on business, he runs straight into his electrifying one-night stand from two years ago. Except Gabi Casas now has twins—his heirs! His childhood as an orphan taught Nate to trust nobody, but he wants better for his sons... so he drops to one knee!

#4189 CONTRACTED AND CLAIMED BY THE BOSS
Brooding Billionaire Brothers
by Clare Connelly

Former child star Paige Cooper now shuns fame and works as a nanny. When Australian pearl magnate and single father Max Stone hires her to help his daughter, she's shocked by her red-hot response to him. And as the days count down on Paige's contract, resistance is futile...

#4190 SAYING "I DO" TO THE WRONG GREEK
The Powerful Skalas Twins
by Tara Pammi

Ani's wedding will unlock her trust fund and grant her freedom—she just doesn't expect infuriatingly attractive Xander at the altar! Penniless, Ani can't afford to walk away. Their craving for each other might be as hot as her temper, but can she risk falling for a man who scorns love?

#4191 A DIAMOND FOR HIS DEFIANT CINDERELLA
by Lorraine Hall

Matilda Willoughby's guardian, ultra-rich Javier Alatorre, is determined to marry her off before her twenty-fifth birthday. Otherwise he must marry her himself! As she clashes with him at every turn, her burning hatred soon becomes scorching need. And Matilda is unprepared for how thin the line between love and hate really is!

#4192 UNDONE IN THE BILLIONAIRE'S CASTLE
Behind the Billionaire's Doors...
by Louise Fuller

Ivo Faulkner has a business deal to close. Except after his explosive night with Joan Santos, his infamous laser focus is nowhere to be found! He invites her to his opulent castle to exorcise their attraction, but by indulging their temptation, Ivo risks being unable to ever let his oh-so-tempting Cinderella go...